NATIONAL BESTSELLING AUTHOR

ROY CLINTON

LOVE CHILD

A MIDNIGHT MARAUDER ADVENTURE

LOVE CHILD

A Midnight Marauder Adventure

Roy Clinton

Published by Top Westerns Publishing (www.TopWesterns.com), 3730 Kirby Dr., Suite 1130, Houston, TX 77098. Contact info@TopWesterns.com for more information.

Book Design by Teresa Lauer: Info@TeresaLauer.com.

Cover by Laurie Barboza DesignStashBooks@gmail.com

Copy Editor: Sharon Smith

Substantive Editor: Maxwell Morelli

Other Books by Roy Clinton

Lost
Midnight Marauder
Return of Midnight Marauder
Revenge of Midnight Marauder
Midnight Marauder and the President of the United States

These books and others can be found on
www.TopWesterns.com and *www.Amazon.com*.
Audio versions of the books can be found on
www.Audible.com as well as on iTunes.

Dedicated to
Dave Ardoin
A good man taken from us too soon
"the Ragin' Cajun"

Table of Contents

PREFACE

February of 1874
BANDERA, TEXAS

M ayor, I don't care if you don't think it's your business. We elected you mayor and we expect you to do something about it!" The part of Slim Hanson's responsibility as mayor he liked the least, was listening to complaints from citizens who felt he was obligated to look into every concern or problem anyone in the town faced.

"Mrs. Mercer, I can understand you and Mrs. Grimes not getting along. But she must live about a mile from your place."

"Actually, it's closer to two miles. But when she comes to town, she takes the wagon road that is right in front of my house. Every time she passes, she sticks her nose in the air and says "Humpf.""

"She says what?"

"Humpf. And I want you to do something about it."

"But Mrs. Mercer, there is not anything against the law about that." How did I get myself roped into this? Trying to reason with her is like trying to reason with that old heifer on the H&F that keeps getting stuck when she sticks her head between the rails of the fence.

Slim continued trying to reason with the disgruntled woman. It did no good to tell her that was not his job or that her neighbor wasn't breaking the law. He figured there was something deeper going on, and as much as he wanted to help, he knew he just didn't have the patience needed to find a solution.

"Mrs. Mercer, you and Mrs. Grimes used to be the best of friends. At least that's how it looked. Any time one of you was in town, I knew I would see the other. You never went anywhere without each other. What happened to that friendship?"

"I'll tell you what happened. Last month at the church social, she baked a pie using my recipe. And she took credit for it!"

"Let me get this straight," said Slim. "Mrs. Grimes baked a pie and took credit for baking the pie?"

"No. She took credit for the recipe."

"Just how did she do that?" Slim could feel his patience coming to an end.

"It was my apple pie recipe she used. Her pies never did come out right. But she used my recipe and when people complimented her on how good the pie was, she just said 'thank you' and let them go on believing it was her recipe."

"Did she actually tell anyone it was her recipe?"

Just then, a teenage boy came walking in the office behind Mrs. Mercer.

"I'll be with you in a minute, son," said Slim as he tried to direct his attention back to the crisis of the moment.

"What did you call me?" asked the boy.

"I didn't call you anything, son. I just said I'd be with you in a minute."

"There, you did it again. Why do you keep calling me son?"

"I'm sorry. I meant no harm. I should've said, 'Young man, I'll be with you in a few minutes.'"

Slim thought, every time I come to town and go to the mayor's office, I face the same thing. People bring their problems to me. And as I try to help, it seems I always offend someone.

"Now what were you saying, Mayor?"

Slim tried to remember what the conversation with Mrs. Mercer was even about. "Did Mrs. Grimes actually tell anyone it was her recipe?"

Mrs. Mercer thought about it for a moment. "No, Mayor, I don't remember her doing that. But she just let people think it was her recipe."

"Mrs. Mercer, maybe Mrs. Grimes just didn't know how to take the compliments she received."

Slim got up from his desk and lowered his voice as he moved closer to Mrs. Mercer.

"Besides everyone in town knows Mrs. Grimes is not that great of a cook and they also know you make the best pie in town. With you bein' neighbors and all, I doubt anyone seriously thought her pie makin' suddenly got that much better. I'll bet everyone at the social was secretly remarkin' at how nice it was for you to lend Mrs. Grimes your recipe."

Mrs. Mercer's face brightened. "Do you really think so?"

"I know so. It's no secret you are might near the best cook in all of Bandera. And you certainly make the best pies anyone's ever tasted. I'd imagine, people all over town are still talkin' about how nice it was for you to help your neighbor so she wouldn't be embarrassed at another social."

"I never thought about it like that, Mayor. You know, I think you're right. Now that I think of it, I saw several of the women smiling at me when Mrs. Grimes was being complimented. Thank you, Mayor. I knew you would have a solution. I'm glad we elected you. Well, I have to go now. Please give my best to Charlotte."

"I will Mrs. Mercer. Thanks for comin' by."

As she was walking out, Marshal Williams walked into the office and went immediately to the stove and poured him a cup of coffee.

"Mornin' Slim," said the marshal.

"Howdy, Marshal.

"What's Mrs. Mercer got a bee in her bonnet about?"

"It seems there was some confusion over who gets the credit for the recipe Mrs. Grimes used last week when she made a pie for the church social," said Slim.

"Thought she was all tuckered out on that by now" said the marshal. "She's been to my office twice this week talkin' about the same thing. I'm just glad you were in town today so she would come talk to you and give me a rest."

"I hope we've heard the end of it. By the way, Clem, did you see that boy that was in my office? He must have left just before you walked in."

"Yup. But don't know his name. He's been hangin' 'round here for the last couple of weeks. I've seen him sweepin' up over at the Cheer Up a couple of times. Last week, he was over muckin' out stalls at the livery. Seems like he's always workin'."

"Any idea where he came from?" Slim asked. "There's somethin' familiar about him but I just can't place it."

"No. He just showed up here one day. Next thing I knew he was workin' for different merchants. He don't seem to be causin' no trouble. Did he cause any trouble here?"

"Oh, it's nothin' like that Clem. He just seemed a might touchy. I was just wonderin' who he was."

Slim and the marshal finished their coffee and walked out of the office when Slim spotted the boy across the street at the Cheer Up. He had a broom in his hand as he walked into the saloon. Slim was sure he must have met the boy before but he couldn't place his name. The boy was about fifteen or sixteen and had very dark brown hair but his eyes were between blue and brown. He had a dark complexion and was already nearly six feet tall. Slim thought he was going to be a big man when he was full grown.

Slim's curiosity got the best of him so he walked over to the Cheer Up and looked over the swinging doors. There were a few cowboys standing at the bar and a few others were sitting down playing cards. Slim spotted the boy in the back of the saloon. He walked over to the boy and called out to him.

"Pardon me, son. You came by my office earlier but didn't wait around. What was it you needed?"

"Why do you keep calling me that? Why do you call me 'son'?"

"I meant no harm. If you tell me your name, I can address you more properly."

"My name is Richie."

Slim stuck out his hand and said, "Pleased to meet you, Richie. You can call me Slim."

Richie shook Slim's hand. "I can't do that. It wouldn't be respectful. I'll just call you mayor."

"That's fine Richie. I like a boy with good manners. Have we met before? I could swear I've seen you before but I don't remember where."

"No. I'm sure we haven't met before."

"Why don't we sit down a talk a bit, son—I mean Richie." The boy propped his broom against the wall and took a seat across the table from Slim.

"Do you live 'round here Richie?"

"I guess I do now. I'm really from Laredo. But I've been here about a month."

"What are you doin' in Bandera? You're a long way from Laredo."

"My mother always told me if something ever happened to her, I was to go to Bandera."

"Did she tell you why she wanted you to do that?" asked Slim.

"No, she just said things would be better for me here if something happened to her. She even said I had some family around here."

"So what happened to your mother, Richie?"

The boy bowed his head and tears fell from his eyes. He placed his head down on the table and continued to weep silently. Slim put his hand on the boy's back and waited. He didn't want to force the boy to talk about something that was painful to him. If the boy wanted to tell him, Slim would be willing to listen. Slowly, the boy raised his head for a moment.

"She died." Richie put his head back on the table and wept so hard that his shoulders were heaving as he cried. Slim pressed his hand a bit harder on the boy's back and rubbed it back and forth. As the boy cried, Slim could feel his grief as he thought of the people he had lost to death, including both of his parents. But his thoughts especially went to Charlotte's mother and how devastated he was when she died.

After several minutes, Richie raised his head. "I'm sorry, mister. I didn't mean to cry like that. It's just that I miss her so much."

"I'm sure you do, Richie. When I've lost someone to death that I love, I always cried."

"But you're a grown man. Men aren't supposed to cry."

"I don't know who told you that, Richie. But grown men do cry. There's nothin' wrong with men cryin'. In fact, cryin' is the most natural thing in the world to do when we get really sad. By the way, why did you come by my office earlier."

"Well, the office has been closed since I got to town. Today was the first time I've seen anyone around it."

"I don't get to town that much," said Slim. "I usually stay out on my ranch. But I come to town every now and then just to check on things and see if I'm needed for any mayor-like duties. So why did you come by to see me?"

"I figured the mayor might help me find a place where I could live."

"Where do you stay now?" asked Slim.

"Mr. Harris over at the livery stable lets me bed down in one of the stalls. All I have to do is to help out by cleaning up after the horses. And Miss Benson pays me two bits a day for sweeping up the saloon. She also feeds me supper. But I think I need to start figuring something out that's more permanent."

"Well, Richie, you can come out to the ranch with me. I can always use a good hand. And it looks like you're not afraid of work. I'll pay you a dollar a day and you can live in the bunkhouse with the other hands. We serve three meals every day. And you can eat all you want."

Richie's face brightened and he wiped his tears on his sleeve. "Thanks, mister. That would be great. I'd like that. But I have to tell you, I don't know anything about working on a ranch. But I'm a quick learner."

"I'm sure you are, Richie. We'll get started to the ranch as soon as you're ready."

"I'm ready now. Can we go now?"

"I don't see why not. We should get there just in time to eat. Do you have a horse?

"Yes, sir. He's over at the livery. First, I need to let Miss Benson know I won't be working here anymore."

"Looks like you can do that now. Here she comes. Hello Nellie. Richie here tells me he's been workin' for you."

"Hello, Slim. I was just coming over to see why you're holding up my employee," she said with a twinkle in her eye. "How's he supposed to get any work done with you talking his ear off?"

"Sorry about that, Nellie. Richie and I were just talking about his future. Isn't that right, Richie?"

"Yes sir. Miss Benson, I'm not going to be working here anymore. I'm going to work on the mayor's ranch."

"You are? Well good for you. That sounds like it will be a lot better job for you. I guess I need to pay you what I owe you."

"No ma'am. You don't owe me anything more. You paid me for my work yesterday and I haven't even worked a half of a day today so you don't owe me anything. I do want to thank you for giving me a job and for being so nice to me."

"You're welcome, Richie. You're a good employee. If ever you decide you want to come back to work here, there'll always be a job waiting for you. You have proven to be a very fine worker."

"Thank you ma'am. Mr. Mayor, I'll go get my horse and be ready to go when you are."

"That's fine, Richie." The boy ran through the saloon and out the doors as he headed to the livery to collect his horse. "Nellie, thanks for bein' so good to Richie. It sounds like he's had a tough go of it since his mother died."

"I was glad to do it, Slim. He's a good boy and he sure works hard. But he'll be better off on the ranch. And I know you will be able to offer him more work and more pay that I can here. There's just not much for him to do other than sweep the floor. And he can only do that so many times a day."

"You're a good woman, Nellie. I appreciate you lookin' out for him."

Slim walked out of the saloon and over to close up his office and get his horse. Richie was already saddled up and waiting in front of Slim's office.

"My but you are a speedy one, Richie. It didn't take you any time to get your horse saddled."

Richie smiled at the compliment. Slim reined his horse around and headed toward the H&F. Once they cleared the last buildings in town, Slim let his horse lope and Richie stayed right by his side. Once they arrived at the ranch, Slim tied his horse to the hitching rail in front of the dining hall and went inside.

"Daddy!" said Charlotte. "We're over here." Charlotte, John, and the twins were seated in the corner and were already eating. "Who's this fine-looking young man you have with you?" asked Charlotte.

"Richie, I would like for you to meet my daughter, Charlotte. And this is my son-in-law, John." John Crudder stood to shake hands with the boy. He looked up at the tall youngster and smiled to himself as he thought what a big man he was going to grow into. "And these are my granddaughters, Cora and Claire. Girls, say hello to Richie."

"Hello," came their reply in unison.

"Richie's mother just died in Laredo. She told him if ever anything happened to her that he was to come to Bandera.

Anyway, I just met him and hired him on at the H&F so you're gonna be seein' a lot of him. Richie, go get you something to eat and come on back and share our table."

"Yes sir," Richie said as he bounded toward the chow line.

"Daddy, he seems like a nice young man. And he sure is cute."

"Hey, hey," said John with a bit of a laugh. "You better be watchin' what you say. Your husband might get jealous."

Charlotte playfully poked John in the ribs. "You know there's no one I think is more handsome than you. And you don't have anything to be jealous about. He's just a boy." John slipped his arm around Charlotte and thought how lucky he was to have her as his wife.

Slim joined Richie in the chow line. When their plates were full they came back to the table and sat down. Slim watched as he quietly bowed his head for a few seconds before eating.

"Richie," asked Charlotte. "What's your full name?"

"My last name's Hanson. But my full name is Richard Hanson, Junior. No one has ever called me Richard. People just call me Richie."

Roy Clinton

CHAPTER 1

Slim's fork slipped from his hand and loudly dropped on to his plate. Charlotte and John looked at each other with their mouths open. Richie kept eating, oblivious to the bomb he had just dropped into the conversation.

"What was your mother's name," asked Slim.

"Marie Hanson."

"What was her full name?" Slim's voice was noticeably louder and had a bit of an edge to it. Richie was startled by his tone but didn't slow down his eating. He was shoveling in food just as quickly as he could.

"Her name was Consuelo Marie de Zavala Morales Hanson."

"What a lovely name," said Charlotte. John and Slim were still too stunned to speak. They just stared at Richie. "Will you tell me about her? Your mother must have been a wonderful woman."

"She was, Charlotte." Richie stopped eating and put his fork down. Tears once again gathered in his eyes has the conversation turned to his mother.

"She was the finest person I know. Mom raised me by herself and didn't have help from anyone. But she never complained. Her own parents didn't want anything to do with her but it didn't matter to her. She made dresses for women in Laredo so we got along just fine." Tears were streaming down his face as he stared at his plate.

"Where was your father," asked Charlotte.

"I don't know. She wouldn't ever talk about him. Any time I asked her about him, all she would say was that he was a good man although her family didn't want him around."

"Did you ever meet your father?" ask Charlotte.

"No. I don't know anything about him other than Mom saying he was a good man."

Charlotte looked at Slim but Slim was looking up at the ceiling.

"Richie," said Charlotte. "I think you and I might be related."

"Really? I don't think I have any family around here. Before my mother said I had some relations here in Bandera, I thought our only relatives was her family in Mexico and we didn't see them very much."

"You see, Richie," Charlotte continued. "My name is Hanson. At least it used to be. I'm Charlotte Crudder now but it used to be Charlotte Hanson. Daddy?" Slim didn't seem to hear Charlotte. She called him again. "Daddy, is there anything you would like to say? I think all of us would enjoy hearing from you."

Slim let out a long sigh, looked at Charlotte, then at John, and then at Richie. "Well, I don't really know how to say this, but Richie, my name is Richard Hanson." He paused and added, "I guess it's really Richard Hanson Senior." There was a pained look on Slim's face as he struggled to continue his response.

"I was in love with your mother before you were born. I asked her to marry me but she got angry and said she couldn't marry me. She didn't tell me why and just said she would never be able to marry me. I wasn't sure how I'd gotten her angry. In fact, I never saw her after that day. That was about sixteen years ago. I didn't know she was expectin' a baby. In fact, I've tried to find her so many times over the past sixteen years but never found out where she was."

Richie stared in disbelief as he listened. Charlotte placed her hand over his. John placed a hand on Richie's back.

"Richie," began Slim. "I'm not sure how to tell you this. But it appears I'm your father. I never knew you existed. If I did, I would have come to you and your mother. I loved her with all of my heart." He turned to Charlotte and continued. "Charlotte, I didn't think it was possible for me to ever love someone again after your mother died. But I met Marie in San Anton when I was coming back from a cattle drive."

There was silence at the table as they waited for Slim to continue his story. Even the twins were quiet. Richie's mouth was open as he stared at Slim.

"Richie, you have to believe me. I would never have done anything to hurt your mother. I loved her. She told me goodbye and said she never wanted to see me again. I was stunned and, I have to admit a bit angry. So I came back to Bandera. But as I tried to make sense of her change in mood toward me, I thought there must be somethin' else goin' on. I went back to San Anton but she had moved. No one knew where she went. I looked for her but couldn't find her. I was even plannin' on going to Mexico to find her parents but I didn't have a clue where they lived. Richie, if I had known about you, I never would have allowed her to drive me away. I hope you believe me."

"I don't know what to believe. But I don't believe you're my father. She would have told me if you were."

"Why do you suppose she wanted you to come to Bandera?" asked Slim.

"I don't know. She never told me except that it would be better for me here and that I had some family here."

"Richie," said Charlotte. "We are the only Hansons in all of Bandera County. That means I'm your sister. At least, I'm your half-sister."

Richie put his hands to his face. Between his fingers, tears began to flow. Charlotte put her arm around him and pulled him into a hug. He put his arms around her and continued to sob. Charlotte, Slim, and John began weeping as well. Cora and Claire looked confused.

"Why's Mommy crying?" asked Claire as she began to sniffle. Cora joined in and tears began flowing from both girls. They didn't know what was wrong but it seems they weren't going to be left out if everyone was crying. Charlotte tried to comfort them. Slim picked up Cora and started patting her on the back and Charlotte picked up Claire. Cora cried louder, "Mommy!" Slim relented and handed Cora to Charlotte. He knew at times like this, even though Charlotte would literally have her hands full with the twins, they could only be comforted by their mother.

Slim stood and walked over to Richie and put out his hand.

"Well, it looks like me calling you 'son' in town was right after all. I guess I really am your father."

Richie looked at Slim's hand and slowly stood up. He started to reach out to take Slim's hand but then threw both of his arms around him.

"Pa! I've always wondered who you were."

"I'm right here, son. And I'll make sure I'm always here for you. You can count on it.

Richie and Slim continued clinging to each other and crying with abandon, as did John and Charlotte. And the twins, who had almost stopped, let out wales that caused all of the hands in the dining hall to stop their eating and stare at the odd happenings.

Soon crying turned to laughing. At first, it was just a little giggle but before long everyone at the table was doubling over with laughter. Even Claire and Cora joined in. Even the confused cowboys that were watching started joined the laughter that was now filling the dining hall. It seemed the happy spirit was infectious.

Roy Clinton

CHAPTER 2

D addy," said Charlotte. "Let's go to the house. It sounds like there's a lot to talk about. We'll be more comfortable there."

The others at the table nodded in agreement. The group got up from the table. John took Cora from Charlotte and Slim took Claire. They walked over to Slim's house and took their places in the spacious living room.

Slim had built the large stone house before Charlotte was born. The room they were in had large windows on two sides, letting in an abundance of light. At one end of the room was a fireplace that was nearly large enough to stand in and not touch the top. When cold descended on Bandera, it was large enough to easily heat the whole house. Slim loved it all the more because of the evenings spent around the fire with Charlotte's mother.

Above the fireplace was a portrait from Charlotte's mother, Leticia Hanson, though Slim always called her Lettie. The furniture in the room was rugged and heavy. Each piece was covered in leather. Colorful pillows were on each couch and the chairs. There was seating for at least twenty. Many times, in years past, all seats were taken as Slim and Lettie entertained their friends from Bandera. Slim also used it regularly for planning meetings with his top hands.

Lettie had decorated the entire house and Slim never changed a thing. When Charlotte was a teen, she introduced some changes to the house that Slim accepted without resistance. But when she wanted to make changes in the living room, Slim wouldn't allow it. He wanted it just the same as when Lettie left it for the last time.

In the center of the room hung a large chandelier. However, the only time it would be lit was when they were having a party. Most evenings, Slim would light the beautiful lamps that adorned each table. The lamps were imported by Lettie from Europe. No one in Bandera had anything to equal their beauty.

Charlotte put on a pot of coffee while the men played with Claire and Cora. Richie, it seemed, had fallen naturally into the role of uncle and perhaps even surrogate brother. The girls laughed as he made silly faces and lifted them high in the air.

"My turn!" said Cora as she watched her sister flying high in the air. He put Claire down and picked up Cora and gave her the same ride.

In a few seconds, Claire said, "My turn!" He did this several times as John and Slim laughed along with the girls. After a few minutes, Charlotte brought in mugs and a pot of coffee and set them in the middle of a large coffee table that was in the center of the room. The table was large enough they didn't have to worry about the girls reaching up and accidently spilling the hot coffee on them.

"Daddy," said Charlotte. "I think we'd all like to hear about you and Marie."

Slim sipped his coffee and gathered his thoughts. After a full minute of silence, he began to speak.

"Yes, there's lots to tell. And I will be glad to tell it. But first, Charlotte, I need you to hear something about your mother."

Charlotte had two hankies in her lap. She seemed sure she would need them both.

"When I married your mother, I was the happiest man alive. I knew the greatest accomplishment of my life to that point and probably for my entire life was to convince her to marry me. We didn't have much but it didn't matter. We bought a piece of land, near where this house is standing, and built a three-room shotgun house. From our perspective, we thought we were wealthy.

"We bought a few head of cattle and all of the calves we could afford and the Hanson Ranch was born. In the first couple of years, we were able to add land to the ranch. Jim Faucett owned the land we now call the Southern end of the ranch. The H&F was born, and we found that together we could be much more prosperous.

"Charlotte, when your mother told me she was carrying you, my love for her grew even greater—though I didn't think that was possible. I began loving you long before I saw you.

"I wanted you and your mother to have a proper place to live so I built this house. I wanted it to be the grandest house in the whole county. Your mother said she didn't need it. But it was her willingness to do without that made me all the more determined to build it.

"I had it completed several weeks before you were due. We had enough hands on the ranch to help out so it didn't take long to build. Meanwhile, your mother set about to order the things that were needed to make the house a home. It took some convincing but I did talk her into ordering the best furniture and furnishings she could find. I felt nothing was too good for my wife and the child she was carrying.

"When it was time for your mother to deliver, I rode into town and brought the doctor back. I was not gone long but while I was out, your mother had delivered you. When the doc and I got to the house, your mother had you lying on her tummy and was gently rubbing your head and back. You were beautiful—perfect in every way. And you never made a sound. It was like you were just glad to be in the world and were taking in your surroundings.

"Your mother was smiling but I could tell she was exhausted. The doctor began to examine your mother and said she had lost a lot of blood." Slim paused and wiped the tears out of his eyes. "Charlotte, your mother never lived long enough to even hold you a second time. I stood by with you in my arms and watched the doc pull a sheet up over your mother's head. Later that afternoon, I buried her. You've been to that little cemetery many times to take her flowers. She loved that little hill so I knew that would be the right spot for her final resting place.

"As much as I loved your mother, I didn't spend a lot of time grieving. I knew my job was to raise you so I gave the entire focus of my life to being the best father I knew how to be."

"And you've been great," said Charlotte. "I couldn't have asked for a better father than you have been to me." She squeezed his hand and Slim continued his story.

"I was certain I would never marry again. No one could take your mother's place. I was sure of that so I hired a nanny to take care of you. Do you remember Mrs. Barnes?"

"Of course, I do. But I never called her anything other than Mrs. B. I remember there were many times when you were out on cattle drives and she stayed here to take care of me."

"That's right. In fact, when you were still small, I realized it would be best to get her to move in so she could take care of you full-time. You remember, she had an upstairs bedroom until you were about ten. By then her health was failing and she wanted to move to Austin to be near her son.

"Anyway, with Mrs. Barnes taking care of you, I was able to go on more cattle drives. I found the beef I raised here would fetch a much higher price in Kansas City. That helped me to get a more solid footing on the ranch.

"In fact, on my last cattle drive, I made enough money to buy out Faucett so the whole H&F would be ours. At the end of that drive, I stopped in San Anton to rest up for a day. Richie, that's when I met your mother. I was walking down the boardwalk too fast and I bumped into her causing her to spill her packages"

"What was she doing in San Antonio?" asked Richie.

"She said she was there to get furnishings for a ranch her family owned in Mexico. Since I watched Lettie furnish this house, I felt I could quickly tell her what I learned. Before I knew it, we'd spent the entire day together looking at furniture and other things for her ranch. I telegraphed Mrs. Barnes and told her I was delayed a couple of days.

"Marie and I spent every available minute together during those days. She was beautiful and had an easy laugh that reminded me of Lettie. I don't really know how to explain it but I fell in love with her." He turned to Charlotte and took her hand. "It was as deep of a love as I had for your mother but I did love her. I'm sorry to tell you that."

"Don't be, Daddy. You didn't do anything wrong. It's all right with me that you fell in love with Marie. I don't think any less of you. That's natural and normal. So, what happened next?"

"Well, I needed to get back to Bandera to check on you but I met Marie in San Anton again the next week and we spent several more days together. After that, she went back to Mexico to tell her parents about the purchases she had made. She sent me a telegram and told me she needed more furniture and she was going back to San Anton.

"I could hardly wait. From her telegram, I knew she was inviting me to join her. I was certain I was in love with her and decided I would ask her to be my wife.

"We had a wonderful time in San Anton. I hadn't been as happy since Lettie was alive. We felt like we were teenagers in love. Those few days I spent with her couldn't have been more perfect."

CHAPTER 3

Actually, they were perfect until I proposed." Slim paused and wiped tears that had once again formed in his eyes. "When I told her I wanted her to be my wife, you would have thought I'd slapped her in the face. She told me she couldn't marry me because her parents would never approve of her marrying a gringo. That's what she called me. A gringo.

"She turned her back on me and started running away. I caught up with her and turned her around and tried to hold her in my arms." Slim mopped more tears from his eyes. "I tried to reason with her but she wasn't hearin' anything I was sayin'. In fact, she started saying hateful and vile things about me. I didn't think she even had those words in her vocabulary.

"I guess she got what she wanted 'cause I got on my horse and rode just as hard as I could for Bandera. The whole way here I was scolding myself for falling in love with a woman who thought so little of me.

"After a few days, I cooled down and it suddenly came to me that she didn't hate me at all. I was sure she loved me as much as I loved her. I realized she said those things to me so I would not press her any more to get married. It was obvious she wanted to honor her parent's wishes and couldn't marry someone who was not a Mexican.

"But I couldn't settle for that. I wasn't going to lose another woman that I loved. So I saddled up and rode to San Anton just as hard as I could. In my mind, I was sure I would find a way to convince her to marry me. But when I got there, I found she'd left town. There was no trace of her anywhere. I went to the stores where she'd bought furniture so I could find out where they shipped it. But in every store, the proprietors told me she had left specific instructions that they were not to allow the shipping address to be divulged to anyone.

"I even went to the freight lines. Surely they'd tell me where in Mexico they delivered the furniture. But again, they told me sternly they would never reveal the address of the shipment.

"Having done all I could to find her, I finally returned to Bandera."

"Did you ever hear from her again?" asked Richie.

"Yes, I did. She sent me a telegram but it didn't say where it was from. She said she was married and had a son and she was sorry for how she had hurt me." Slim paused and dipped his head. Tears were flowing. "Then she told me she did indeed love me but knew we could never get married because of her family. She wished me success and happiness and that was the last I've heard from her. I still have the telegram and read it again every so often and I still dream of what might have been."

Richie said, "I don't think Mom ever married. She had the name

Hanson all my life. Besides telling me you were a good man, the only other thing she told me was the two of you couldn't live together because of her family. I've seen the family tree in her Bible. She had Richard Hanson, Senior listed as my father."

"Richie," said Slim. "I'm so sorry I didn't know about you. If I had, I would have found a way to convince your mother to marry me. We might not have been accepted by her parents but we would have been happy together."

"You know the ironic thing, Pa?" A big smile spread across Slim's face as he heard his son acknowledge him as his father. "Her parents wouldn't accept her anyway because they said she had a gringo half-breed for a son."

Slim's eyes narrowed into slits and he took a deep breath. "What kind of people would turn their back on their own daughter? I'm sorry to say this about your grandparents, Richie, but I think they must have been mean people to treat you and your mother that way."

"Richie," said Charlotte. "Tell us more about your life. I want to hear about your mother and how the two of you got along."

Richie turned pensive and thought for a few minutes and then started to speak about his childhood.

Roy Clinton

CHAPTER 4

LAREDO, TEXAS

H ey Ma," shouted Richie. "Why can't I have a pony like the other kids?"

"Now, Richie," Marie replied, "You know I'd get you one if I could afford it. But we just don't have enough money to spend on things we don't really need. Besides, you can ride the buggy horse anytime you'd like."

"But Ma, it's not the same. We don't even have a saddle for the old nag." Richie stomped through the house showing his displeasure over his mother's words.

It was certainly difficult raising a son by herself. Marie was able to keep them in a rented house in town and put food on the table from the money she made as a dressmaker. He reputation was widely known throughout Laredo. There was no shortage of work but even working seven days a week, she made just enough for her and her son to survive.

When she was expecting Richie, she took a buggy back to her

home near Monterey in Old Mexico. By the time she arrived, it was obvious she was going to have a baby. Her parents shamed her and said she had brought disgrace on the family. They talked a lot about their station in life and how the Mexican Aristocracy, as they put it, were above such behavior. They told her she could stay the night but after that she was to leave and never return.

Marie traveled back to Texas settled in Laredo because it was the first town in the United States she came across after leaving Mexico. She thought about returning to San Antonio and letting Slim know about her condition. But she feared he would also see her as a fallen woman just as her parents had.

Richie was born just a few days after arriving in Laredo. She was grateful that her mother had given her enough money to survive for a few months after his birth. But she knew she would have to find a job or some way to make a living. She didn't see how she could work and still care for Richie.

The only skill she had that she felt was marketable was her sewing. From an early age, Marie had made all of her own clothes. She even made clothes for her mother and father. As an only child, her parents doted on her and expressed great pride in her skills as a seamstress.

In Laredo, she hung out a sign on her porch that simply said, "Experienced Seamstress. Ladies Dresses Custom Made." Since her rented house was on the main road at the edge of town, many people passed it. It wasn't long before she had all of the work she could manage while still being able to take care of Richie and play with him each day.

The school was almost directly across the street from her house. When Richie started school at age five—a whole year earlier than the other children—she could watch him from the time he left her house until he was inside the schoolhouse. Richie was a good student and really enjoyed studying and learning. Marie impressed on him that his education was the key to being able to do anything with his life he wanted.

Being younger than the other kids, Richie had his share of bullying. Marie wished he had a father who could teach him how to take care of himself. The best she could do in teaching him to defend himself was to tell him to run straight home just as fast as he could if someone started to mistreat him. That earned him the reputation of being a momma's boy, a moniker he carried until he was about ten.

By age ten, Richie was a whole head taller than the other boys his age. Actually, he was taller than most boys in school. One of the boys who had bullied Richie throughout the previous five years started picking on Richie again. But this time, Richie doubled up both fists and hit the boy several times in the face. Richie got sent home from school because fighting was against the rules. However, as soon as the other students were dismissed, the teacher came to tell Marie what had happened.

"Mrs. Hanson, I'm sorry I had to send Richie home from school today. He knows fighting is strictly against the rules." The teacher paused as Richie entered the room. "But Richie, I want you to know I'm proud of you. You taught that bully a lesson. He's been picking on you for years. And I don't think he will ever pick on you again. After word gets around to how you took care of him, I doubt you will have any problem with anyone else."

Richie smiled as his mother hugged him and the teacher excused herself to return to the schoolhouse. Marie was proud of the young man he had become. She started thinking about her parents in Mexico and wondered if they would change their minds about her and Richie and see the error of their ways.

When school dismissed for the summer, Marie and Richie loaded their buggy and headed out to Mexico. Monterrey was about an eight-day trip. The summer heat was relentless but Richie never complained. They looked forward to being able to cool off in the shade of the trees surrounding the ranch where Marie had lived until she became pregnant.

They arrived at the ranch and were warmly greeted by several of the workers. Richie climbed down and put his hands on his mother's waist to help her down. Just as Marie's feet touched the ground, her mother appeared in the doorway and shouted, "What do you think you are doing? Get back in that wagon and leave here immediately."

"Mother," pleaded Marie, "I want you to meet your grandson. This is Richie." Richie pulled off his hat and took steps toward his grandmother.

"You stop right there. You are not my grandson. You're a gringo half-breed." Then she turned to Marie and using all of the venom she could muster said, "And you are not my daughter. Leave here at once or I will have you thrown out."

Richie set his jaw and doubled up his fists. Marie took him by the shoulder and turned him toward her. "She's not worth it, son." Then addressing her mother, Marie continued, "You will never see either of us again."

They climbed in the buggy and Richie turned it back to the road they had just traveled. "Why do they hate us so much?" asked Richie.

"Because she can't stand the thought I would ever love your father since he was white. Her hatred for me has poisoned her mind. She will not allow herself the possibility of getting to know you, much less loving you because of her racial hatred."

Marie turned to Richie as he continued driving the buggy off of the ranch and back to the main road. "Richie, don't ever look down on someone because of the color of their skin or because they are in any way different from you. I think the fact that everyone does not look alike makes the world a much nicer place. Just think how dull it would be if every boy looked like you and every woman looked like me."

Richie laughed. His mother had a way of explaining things so that they made sense. That simple lesson would serve him well for the rest of his life.

Roy Clinton

CHAPTER 5

Richie had just turned fifteen and completed his education in Laredo. He thought about going to college as his mother wanted him to but thought he would take a few months off and work so he would have money for school. Marie told him that was not necessary since he had gotten a full academic scholarship to Baylor University in Independence, Texas.

But Richie wanted to stay a few months longer and had hoped to be able to help his mother with some of her living expenses. One afternoon, as he was coming home from his job at the dry goods store, he heard some commotion in the house. As he opened the front door, he saw a man slap his mother and yell, "Where is it? Where's your money?"

The man was tall and thickly built. He wore a tan shirt and a dark brown hat that was so deeply creased that the brim came up high on the sides and pulled down sharply in the front. The top part of the man's right ear was missing and there was a scar from his ear down his cheek.

Richie started for the man when the stranger pulled a gun and shot Marie in the chest. The man released his hold on her and she fell to the ground. Richie went to his mother's side to try to help her.

"Ma! Ma! You're going to be all right. Mother! Mother!"

As he was shouting, the intruder hit Richie in the face with his gun, slipped out of the house, mounted a horse, and galloped away.

Richie was stunned by the blow but retained consciousness. He picked up his mother's head and cradled it in his arms.

"Ma!" said Richie, through tears that were streaming down his face. Richie knew his mother's life was over. She was not breathing and her eyes were still open but not focused on anything. He wept bitterly as he held his mother's head in his lap.

"No!" shouted a woman from the door. Richie turned and saw the woman who lived next door. "No! Marie. Tell me she's all right." She ran to her body and cried without restraint. "Somebody killed Marie. Why would they do that? Marie never hurt anyone?"

She moved over to Richie and took him in her arms. "Poor Richie. Why would anyone hurt your mother?" Richie continued crying and holding his mother's head. A few minutes later the sheriff came in looking for the source of the gunshot. He pulled Richie away from his mother.

"Richie, what happened here?"

"He killed her, sheriff! That man killed Ma."

"Who killed her, Richie?"

"Someone I've never seen before. It was a big man that was missing part of his ear and had a scar on his face."

"That sounds like Holloway. Jasper Holloway. Is that who did it?"

"I don't know sheriff. I don't know his name. All I know is he was shouting for Ma to tell him where she kept her money and then he shot her. Why would he do that? Ma didn't have much money. Everyone knew we were poor. Why would anyone want to hurt her?"

Richie continued to cry as neighbors gathered at the door to see what all of the commotion was about. Over the next few minutes, the undertaker came to come get Marie's body and the priest from the neighborhood church arrived. When Richie saw the priest he ran to him and hugged him.

"Someone killed my ma, Father. Why would anyone want to hurt her?"

"My son, I do not have the answer to that question. All I know is your mother is with God. She is all right. Richie, we are the ones who are hurting now. But your mother is not hurting. She feels no pain."

Richie continued clinging to the priest with his tears flowing down the back of the old man's robe. "You cry all you need to, my son. I am here for you. And the whole congregation is here for you. We loved your mother very much. The two of you were at mass every week. I know she is with God now."

The rest of the day was a blur for Richie. His thoughts vacillated from anger toward Holloway for murdering his mother, to fear about how he would make it in life without her, to uncertainty about what he was going to do in the future. The sheriff and the priest took care of the funeral arrangements. Richie agreed for his mother to be buried the next day in the Camposantantos Cemetery, which meant Saint's Fields.

After the funeral, Richie's thoughts turned toward finding the man responsible for ending his mother's life. Richie found out he was a former drifter who had moved to town about three months earlier. No one knew much about him or where he came from. But he was known for cheating at cards and getting into gunfights— all of which he won.

Richie didn't know the first thing about tracking someone or where to start looking for Holloway. His mother had an old rifle. He had only shot it a few times and knew he was no marksman. Richie went to the livery and traded the buggy and buggy horse for a saddle horse complete with rigging. The proprietor made no secret of the fact that the horse was rather old and couldn't be ridden but a few miles a day. But Richie didn't have enough money to buy a better horse. He needed to use the money he had to find Holloway.

After about a week of aimless wandering and asking if anyone had seen Holloway, he decided the only thing he could do was head to Bandera. He recalled his mother telling him if anything ever happened to her, he was to go there because he had some relatives in the area.

CHAPTER 6

BANDERA, TEXAS

J ohn Crudder listened to the account of the murder of Marie Hanson, he became visibly agitated. Charlotte saw the change in him and knew he was thinking it was time for him to step in. She laid her hand on John's knee and turned to Richie.

"It sounds like you had a wonderful childhood, Richie," said Charlotte. "I'm sorry your mother got killed. That must have been so hard on you."

Richie's eyes filled with tears. He looked over at Slim and saw he was crying hard as well. Silent sobs emanated from both of them.

"I'm so glad you came here and found us," said Charlotte. "We will always be your family. Nothing will ever change that."

"Richie, I know I said you would bed down in the bunkhouse. But that was before I knew you were my son. Charlotte," Slim continued. "Would it be all right with you if Richie moves into your old room?"

"Of course it will, Daddy. I don't use the room any more and it will be perfect for Richie. Well, it's almost perfect. I think we need to do something about yellow walls and the frilly curtains. And I don't think a canopy bed is fitting for a young man like Richie."

"It's settled then," said Slim. "Richie, this afternoon, we will get you moved into your room. Charlotte, would you mind going to town later and ordering a proper bed for him?"

"Of course I don't mind, Daddy."

"And get some paint that is more masculine. And while you're at it, get whatever else he will need to make this his home."

Richie smiled in disbelief. How could he have so many changes have taken place in just one day? He found his father. Discovered he had a sister and a brother-in-law. And even found out he was an uncle and had two adorable nieces.

As Claire and Cora played chase, Charlotte took Slim to her old bedroom so she could tell him of the changes she wanted to make. Slim knew it was a waste of time for him to listen. He didn't have an eye for decorating but Charlotte was like her mother. She instinctively knew exactly what needed to be done. Slim's job was to utter things like, "That's a great idea," and "I'm so glad you thought of that."

John and Richie kept their seats and nursed their cups of coffee that had long since gotten cold. Richie could tell John had something on his mind but he wasn't sure what so he just continued to fain interest in the coffee.

Finally John spoke. "What all did you find out about Holloway?"

"Nothing really other than what I've said. He seemed to be a no-account drifter when he showed up in Laredo. I couldn't find anyone who even knew if he had any friends. It seems he just appeared one day and started playing cards and drinking in the saloon. They say he was loud and mean and when anyone accused him of cheating—and that evidently happened a lot—he would sucker the poor man who accused him into a gunfight and kill him."

John continued asking questions about Holloway. He was also interested in what Richie had found out while he was trying to track him.

"When I went to the sheriff's office, I found there was a wanted poster on Holloway. The sheriff said he hadn't noticed the poster because he and so many other posters of outlaws."

"What was he wanted for," asked John.

"The poster said cattle rustling and horse theft. The sheriff said only real lowlife people steal cattle and horses."

"He had that right," said John. "Were you able to keep the wanted poster?"

"No. I wanted to but the sheriff said it was the only one he had and he needed to keep it."

"Richie, I want you to think hard and tell me everything you can remember about the man who killed your mother."

Richie thought for several seconds. "The first thing I noticed was he was Mexican. That's not much help in Laredo since most people there have skin much darker than mine."

"That's good," said John. "What else did you notice? How tall was he? What was he wearin'?"

"Well, I guess he was a bit taller than me and I'm near about six foot."

"What about his face? Was there anything that stood out to you?"

"Only that he looked real mean. He had kind of a sneer on his face. I could tell he hadn't shaved in a while but his beard was not thick. It had gaps in it and his mustache was real scrawny."

"Did he have any distinguishing marks? Anything that could help identify him?"

"He was missing part of his ear and he had a scar down his face." Richie paused. "But it looked like he had a spider on his hand. I looked at him holding the gun on Ma, and it looked like a spider had crawled up his hand."

"Was it a spider, Richie, or did it just look like a spider?"

"Oh it was a spider all right but it looked like it had been drawn on his hand."

"You mean like a tattoo?" asked John.

"Yeah, that's what it was. It was a tattoo all in black. It was a spider on his hand."

"What hand was he holdin' the gun in?"

"I'm pretty sure it was his left hand."

"Concentrate, Richie. This is really important. Are you sure it was his left hand?"

Richie paused and then said, "Yes, I'm sure. It was his left hand."

"And the spider was on that hand?"

"Yes. I know it was."

"Good, Richie. Just a few more questions. Do you remember the gun belt he was wearing?"

"Yes, I'll never forget that. He had a star on his holster that was made out of silver. It was reflecting the light when I found him hurting Ma."

"Was the holster on his left side or his right side?"

"Well, it was on his left side. Isn't that where holsters are when someone shoots left handed?" Richie seems a little peeved at John's question. It was like John was testing him or something.

"I'm not doubting you, Richie. I just wanted to make sure he was not right handed and just swapped the gun to his left hand."

Richie settled down as he realized John was indeed on his side. Richie continued to scour his memory. "There was something funny about his hat. It had a bunch of notches that were cut into the brim on the right side. At first, I thought it was just an old hat and it was just worn out. But as I think about it, the notches were put there intentionally. He cut them in there. Why do you suppose he did that?"

"I don't know Richie. I know some gunfighters put notches in the grip of their gun for every man they kill. Maybe Holloway was doing the same but only on his hat. Perhaps he wanted everyone to see what a desperado he was."

"He was a bad man, John. Why are you asking me so many questions about him?"

"Richie, someone has to bring him to justice. I used to be a marshal and I seem to have some pretty good skills at tracking down outlaws. I plan to go to Laredo and find Holloway and see that he pays for what he did to you and to your mother."

"Good," said Richie. "And I'm going with you."

"No you're not. I work alone. The only way to catch someone who is on the run is to outsmart them and to sneak up on them."

"But I can help you," pleaded Richie. "I know what he looks like. I'll be able to spot him easily."

"And thanks to the very detailed description you have given, I'll be able to find him as well."

CHAPTER 7

Charlotte and Slim came out of the bedroom. Both had smiles on their faces so it was obvious a plan had come together. Charlotte had a pencil and was making notes about their decisions. As they sat down, they could tell something serious had transpired between John and Richie.

Charlotte turned to John and said, "Out with it. You have that look on your eye like you are getting ready to take a trip. I've seen it many times before. Where're you going, John."

"I think I'll just mosey down to Laredo and nose around a bit. I'd like to find out where Holloway went."

"That's a good idea," said Slim. "And I'm goin' with you. Just give me time to pack us some food for the trip."

"Now, Slim, you can't go and if you'll think about it, you know why."

"Why?" said Slim with a raised voice and red face. He was visibly angry.

"Just think about it, Slim. You're too close to this. Your anger at someone killing Marie will impact your judgment. Anger doesn't mix with guns and rational decision makin'."

Slim slowly cooled down, knowing John was right. He got up and paced a bit which seemed to settle him down.

"When are you leaving, John?" asked Charlotte.

"Right now seems as good of a time as any. I need to get there before Holloway's trail is completely cold."

Charlotte moved over to John and he stood and enveloped her in his arms. Not ever wanted to be left out of a hug, Claire and Cora each hugged John's legs. John knew he was the luckiest man in the world to have the family he did.

He left Slim's house and went out to the corral to saddle Midnight. Meanwhile, Charlotte left the twins with Slim and Richie and went down the path to the home John had built for them on the Medina River. She went out to the smokehouse and got a side of bacon and some beef jerky. When John had his horse saddled, he walked Midnight over to the hitching rail in front of his house, swung down and grabbed his saddlebags.

Inside the house, Charlotte was busily gathering the rest of his supplies. She was sure to pack flour, salt, coffee, and a frying pan. Charlotte also folded several cotton cloths, a small bottle of ointment, and a bottle of whisky. She knew John might need these things if he was injured.

John walked into the kitchen and slipped his arms around her from behind as she continued the preparations for his trip. Finally, she turned around and fell into his embrace.

"Oh, John. I don't know what I would do if anything happened to you. You will be careful, won't you?"

"Of course I will, Charlotte. I will not take any unnecessary risks. You know I'll make wise decisions. I have you and the girls waitin' for me and I'll not let anything keep me from returning to you."

"I just get so afraid," said Charlotte. "Any time you go out of town, I find myself wondering if you'll return."

"Now, now, Charlotte. Don't fret over me. I'll be careful. But if you're that concerned, would you rather that I didn't go?"

Charlotte paused and considered what he asked. She was tempted to ask him to stay and let someone else find the murderer of Richie's mother. "No, John. I know you have to go. And that's one of the things I love about you. I knew as soon as we heard that Marie was murdered, you would be going to catch the killer. There was no doubt in my mind. It's just that I get worried when I think of the danger I know you will face. Remember, I know something about that danger. I lived in the middle of it for several weeks."

John recalled how Charlotte had been kidnapped in hopes of forcing Slim to sell the H&F. All three of them had gotten injured and a lot of people got killed as John took on the entire Bandera Town Council—murderers all—in order to bring Charlotte home again. Charlotte had even pulled the trigger herself to kill the last of the kidnappers.

"I remember, Charlotte. How could I ever forget how close I came to losing you? At the same time, we both know if I don't go, Marie's murderer may never be found. It seems I have gotten pretty good at finding outlaws. And I've learned how to protect myself. Rest assured, I'll not take more risks than are necessary."

"Somehow that doesn't comfort me much. I don't know if you

even know the limit of the risks you will take to balance the Scales of Justice."

John placed a hand on each of Charlotte's cheeks and kissed her tenderly. He continued holding her cheeks and moved back a bit so he could look at her. There were tears flowing down her cheeks onto his hands. He pulled her close and kissed her again and then put his arms around her and hugged her tightly.

When he finally broke the embrace, Charlotte turned and filled his saddlebags with the supplies she had gathered. She walked past John and out the front of the house and placed the saddlebags on Midnight. John followed Charlotte, took the reins and walked with her back to Slim's house.

"Slim," said John. "I've got a general idea where Laredo is but I've never been to Laredo before."

Richie spoke up. "I can help with that, John. The road is called the El Camino Real. It goes all the way down into Mexico. Remember I just came from there. First you go due south until you get to Hondo. Then you continue…."

Richie gave very detailed directions to John even telling him the location of rivers, streams, and lakes. There was a bit of pride in Richie's voice as he contributed the needed information. "Richie," said Slim. "I'm glad you are here. I could have gotten John to Laredo but I didn't remember all of the watering holes."

John turned to Richie and held out his hand. Richie took it as John looked at him eye to eye. "I'm dependin' on you to watch out for my family while I'm gone. Slim does a good job of seein' after Charlotte and the girls. You help him with that—and you watch out for Slim."

Richie grinned, "Yes sir. I'll take good care of them."

John hugged the twins and then swung up into the saddle. Midnight immediately went into a gentle lope. This was the first long ride John had taken since coming back from his meeting with the President a few weeks earlier. Midnight was ready to run. Once they got about a mile from John's house, he gave Midnight his head and let him run flat out for about thirty minutes. While John enjoyed the ride, he was also somber. He didn't know what was waiting for him when he got to Laredo.

CHAPTER 8

Slim took Cora and headed back into his house. Richie picked up Claire and followed. Charlotte remained on the porch and watched as John rode away. For some reason, she had a foreboding of great danger to John. She knew he could handle himself well in the face of danger. But there was something about this time that seemed different. She couldn't put her finger on what she was feeling—only that she felt he was facing greater danger than he had ever encountered.

"Charlotte," shouted Slim from inside the house. "The girls are calling for their mother. There's only so much two men can do for 'em."

Charlotte snapped out of her gloomy thoughts and went inside. "All right. Which of you girls is giving Grandpa problems?"

"Me," said Cora as she held up her hand.

"Me too," said Claire. She copied her sister and raised her hand.

Charlotte laughed and bent down to gather both girls into her arms. "Then we'll just have to do something about that. I think maybe I'll make cookies. Who wants to help me?"

Again the twins erupted in unison. "Me, me. Let me help!"

"I want to help too," said Richie. "I used to help Ma make cookies. I'm pretty good at it."

"I guess I want to help too," said Slim. "I'd hate to be left out."

"Well come on in, all of you. We'll make some cookies."

"Yeah," came the shouts of the twins.

"First, everyone put on an apron." Charlotte opened a drawer containing the aprons. The handed the girls the miniature aprons she had made for them. Richie put his apron on without comment. But Slim groaned as he put his on.

"Now line up at the wash basin. I want everyone to wash your hands. You know what they say. 'Cleanliness is next to godliness.'"

"I don't know who said that but that can't be right," said Slim. Richie smiled as he got to see some of his father's personality coming out. "You'd think it was enough that I put on an apron."

The twins laughed for they were well acquainted with the playful gruffness of Slim. "Who's that laughin' at me?" asked Slim in his biggest pseudo-grumpy voice. "I think I'll just have to tickle anyone who laughs."

He started toward the twins who laughed all the more and then started screaming and running from him as he chased them around the kitchen. When he caught them, he picked up one girl in each arm and growled as he pretended to bite them on their stomachs.

Richie laughed, as did Charlotte. After a few minutes, Slim put the girls down and said, "My hands are now clean and I have on an apron. When are we gonna make cookies?"

"Let me help," shouted the twins in unison.

"Everyone can help," said Charlotte. "Richie, I need you to get one cup of butter and mix it with one and a half cups of sugar. There are measuring cups on that cabinet and you can use a wooden spoon to mix it. It will take a little while to get the two ingredients creamed together."

"I remember. This is exactly the way Ma made cookies."

"Daddy, I need you to get one egg and beat it. The eggbeater is in the cabinet with the measuring cups. And girls, you have the most important job. Come help me measure out a little less than three cups of flour."

Charlotte had previously gotten Slim to make little platforms for each girl so they could help in the kitchen. There was a railing around each platform and three small steps. When she put the platforms in place, the girls stood beside their mother at the counter and began the very messy task of measuring flour and placing it in a bowl. Charlotte would pour the flour and the twins would make sure the measuring cup was full. One of them would level off the top of the cup with a knife and the other would pour it into the bowl. They repeated this process three times, counting off each cup as they progressed.

"Now I need you girls to help me add a spoon of baking powder and a pinch of salt."

Claire plunged her hand into the saltbox and grabbed a handful before Charlotte could stop her and put it into the bowl with the flour. "I think that may be a little too much, sweetheart." Charlotte carefully removed the salt crystals from the flour. She got out all she could see and knew there would still probably be so much salt it might ruin the cookies.

"Cora," Charlotte directed. "I need you to put Grandpa's egg in the bowl with Richie's butter and sugar. Claire, ask Grandpa to get the vanilla extract out of the cupboard and you can add just a few drops to the same bowl." Claire grabbed the bottle and headed to the cookie bowl. Charlotte caught her just in time and guided her hand so she didn't overdo it.

"Now, Richie, I need you to add the dry ingredients to your bowl and mix it all well. It will take a few minutes. Daddy, while he's doing that, please add some more wood to the stove. I want the oven to get a bit hotter. Now the fun part. I'm going to put a bit of grease on the cookie sheet and then I want everyone to come get a small spoon of cookie dough and roll it into a ball and place it on the pan."

All five gathered around the counter and rolled the dough and placed the balls as Charlotte instructed. When the pan was filled, she placed it in the oven. "Daddy, I need you to keep time. I need you to tell us when ten minutes have passed."

Slim pulled his new watch from his pocket and checked the time. As he did, he reflected on how proud he was to receive it from his son-in-law just a few weeks earlier. At the time, he recalled thinking of John as the son he never had. Now just a few days later he had two sons.

The twins went back to playing chase around the kitchen table. Richie and Slim took a seat at the table while Charlotte went to the milk bucket and poured five glasses. She set them on the table and sat down with her father and her brother.

When the cookies were done she served them up to the delight of her daughters. Slim and Richie nodded their approval, stuffed their mouths and went back for seconds. Having eaten their fill, Charlotte directed them to make two more pans of cookies to use up the remaining dough. By the time they finished, it seemed as if Richie had always been part of her life. As she listened to Slim and Richie talk, she thought life just couldn't get any better.

Roy Clinton

CHAPTER 9

EL CAMINO REAL

J ohn let Midnight continue at a fast pace as he headed south. The first leg of his journey was very familiar to him. He had been to Hondo several times since the H&F stretched south to just outside of the town. Crudder marveled at the size of the ranch. It was nearly twenty-five miles from north to south.

Just before dusk, John arrived at the bunkhouse that served as the southern headquarters of the ranch. In reality, it was little more than a large line shack that would sleep up to ten hands at a time. John unsaddled Midnight and gave him a good brushing. He let him roam knowing his stallion would not stray far.

After building a fire, John cooked some bacon and made a pot of coffee. He was grateful Charlotte had included some biscuits that were left-over from breakfast. With supper finished, John sat by the dying fire and watched the sky become increasingly filled with stars and was struck at how full the sky seemed. He still marveled at how many stars he could see in Texas. As a child in

New York, he knew he saw some stars but there seemed to be a long distance between them. But in Texas, it seemed like the stars were on top of each other. On especially dark nights, it looked like the stars were painted as great white swatches across a black velvet background.

At age twenty-nine, John had experienced more than many people would in an entire lifetime. He didn't know what to expect over the next several days. John had little doubt he would encounter danger—it seemed part and parcel of every adventure. Perhaps that was a strange way to think about his travels, calling them adventures but that is the way he saw them. Each time he set out to right a wrong, he considered the episodes as adventures. On each one, he would stand up against evil and, as a result, would be called on to put himself in harm's way.

When John finally left the fire to go inside, there were only embers left. He went into the bunkhouse and lit a lamp. Selecting a bunk, he removed his boots and gun belt and settled into the mattress feeling sure it was his last night in a bed until he found the murderer of Marie. He tossed and turned for hours. It seemed he would sleep for a few minutes and then wake up. Several hours later, as he finally drifted into sound sleep, he dreamed.

'Hold it right there,' I said. 'I'll shoot if you don't drop your gun.' Instead, the masked man shot at me over and over and ran out the door. I gave chase and tried to catch him. When I got outside, he was waiting for me. He raised his gun and shot me in the chest. As I fell to the ground, he walked over to Midnight and shot him in the head. Midnight fell to the ground and the masked man stood over him and shot him again. The gunman laughed and continued to shoot.

'No! No! No! Don't shoot him again. He didn't do anything to you!' I tried to get up but blood was running from the wound in my chest. I knew I would be dead in a few minutes. 'I'm sorry Midnight. I couldn't stop him. Please forgive me.'

John woke up, grabbed his gun from his holster and sat up in bed as he looked for the masked man. It took a few seconds for his head to clear and to realize he had been having a nightmare. He opened the door and saw Midnight standing just a few feet away. The huge horse let out a gentle whinny as though he was assuring John he was safe.

Looking up at the sky, John estimated it was only about an hour until dawn. There was no reason to go back to bed. Sleep was over. He pulled on his boots and strapped on his gun belt. John stoked the fire and heated up the left-over coffee. When the fire was blazing, he roasted a bit of bacon and had two more of the biscuits Charlotte had packed for him.

"Well boy, I'm sure glad to see you're all right."

Midnight whinnied again.

"For a few minutes I thought we were both done for." Midnight moved a bit closer to the fire so John got up and patted the great horse on the neck. It only took a few minutes for John to get him saddled and to put out the fire. Mounting Midnight, he kept the steed to a walk as he waited for the sky to lighten.

Taking the road south, John planned to make it as far as possible before he stopped for dinner. Somewhere around midday, John saw a house not far from the road and what looked like the beginnings of a town. He pulled up to the hitching rail in front of a non-descript building that had a porch that ran the length of the unpainted building. There were several chairs on the porch and a large barrel that could have been filled with pickles, crackers, or any one of several items. One of the chairs was filled with an old man who was snoozing. At his feet was a dog that was sound asleep.

John swung down and said, "Howdy."

"Howdy back to you," said the old man. The dog opened its eyes without ever moving its head. It looked at John for a moment and closed it eyes again.

"I wonder if you have any food inside. I'd sure like to buy something to eat if you have it."

"Of course I do, youngster," said the old man. "I've got just 'bout anything you can think of inside."

John smiled to himself as he considered the statement of the old man. While he might have a nice stock of goods, John didn't think there would be much inside to brag about.

But the store was filled with items of all kinds. There were blankets and various clothing items. There were pots and pans, cooking utensils, farm implements, assorted hardware items including nuts and bolts, tools of every variety, wagon parts, bridles, saddles and other tack, windmill parts—from the looks of things, the proprietor did seem to have just about everything.

John went to a section of the store that was stacked high with canned goods. There was a good stock of vegetables and fruit, soups in several varieties, beef, lamb, and a number of things John had not seen outside of New York, like canned oysters. He smiled to himself as he thought about how he thought the old man was simply bragging.

"What's the name of this community?"

"You are right now standin' in the heart of Nicksville. I'm John L. Nicks and this is my store. I'm also the justice of the peace and the postmaster. Some people 'round here call me mayor but that ain't right."

John smiled to himself. "Pleased to make your acquaintance, Mr. Nicks. My name's John Crudder. You were shor tellin' me straight about your store. You have might near everything in here."

The old man nodded and pursed his lips a bit as though to say, "Told you so, John."

John got a can of beans and a can of peaches and then took a handful of soda crackers from a barrel and placed his selections on the counter. The old man looked at the items and said, "That'll be half a dollar." John put a fifty-cent piece on the counter when the old man continued. "Want me to open those for you?" He pulled a can opener from under the counter and proceeded to open both cans as John nodded his approval. "You can eat out on the porch with me and Blue."

Outside, John took a seat and the old man went back to his chair and shouted at his dog. "Get out of the way, Blue!" The dog lazily got up and moved about two feet away and dropped back to the porch, seemingly asleep before as soon as he landed.

John took a spoon from his saddlebag and ate the beans and

crackers. For dessert he enjoyed the luxury of the canned peaches. He recalled when he was in New York and later in Boston, he hadn't thought of peaches as being special. Since coming to Texas, he had fallen in love with the fruit. Savoring each bite, John tried to carry on a conversation with the old man.

"Mr. Nicks, how long you been here in Nicksville?"

"I'm just Nicks. No mister to it. I've been here nigh onto twenty years. I was the first settler in these parts. Then every few years, others moved in. Don't know why anyone would want to live anywhere else."

John continued eating his peaches and waited to see if Nicks had more to add. There was only silence so John said, "It does look like a nice place to live." The old man just rocked and said nothing more. John finished his peaches, got up and nodded at the old man. "Much obliged, Nicks. I'll probably be seein' you again when I ride back through."

"Stop anytime, youngster. I've got plenty of things to choose from. Next time, you might find you need something more than just a couple of cans of food."

"You may be right about that. Thanks again." John swung up and turned Midnight south. Midnight broke into a run just a few yards from the store and continued running until John reined him in about twenty minutes later. For the rest of the afternoon, John alternated between a gentle lope and holding Midnight to a walk.

John got into Moore a couple of hours later and watered Midnight at the well near the center of town. There was no activity in town other than a couple of dogs that followed Midnight to the water trough. John saw a few saddled horses in front of what looked to be a saloon but there was no other evidence of life.

Riding out of Moore, John saw a sign that said Frio City was thirteen miles ahead. Looking at the sky, he knew he could easily make it by nightfall. While he didn't know anything about the city, it sounded like he might actually be able to have another night sleeping in a bed.

Just before dark, John rode into Frio City. He passed a large stone courthouse, a café and a rooming house. At the end of town John went to the livery stable. John swung down and unsaddled Midnight. He gave his horse a good brushing and arranged for him to have a bucket of oats and asked to have him saddled at first light.

He walked to the café and ordered a beefsteak and cup of coffee. While the food was good, it was not nearly as good as Charlotte's cooking. After supper, he went next door and got a room for the evening.

Just before dawn, John went back to the café and ordered sausage and a couple of fried eggs. At the livery stable, he found Midnight saddled and waiting out front. John paid the stable owner and continued his journey south.

By noon, John was in Darlington. He rode up to the general store and went inside to look for something to eat. Anticipating another wonderful selection of canned goods, he was disappointed to find they only had canned beans and soup. While the store didn't have any crackers, they did have a pickle barrel. John selected a can of beans and fished a pickle from the barrel. It didn't take but a few minutes to eat. After watering Midnight, he continued south toward Cotulla.

As it turned out, Cotulla was actually a large cattle ranch instead of a town. John rode out to the ranch house late in the afternoon. It looked to him like the hands were gathering for supper. John swung down and asked for the ranch foreman.

"I'm Joe," came a voice behind him. John turned around to see a medium height man with dark brown skin, wearing a dirty shirt and a rumpled hat. He appeared to be about John's age or maybe just a bit older. "How can I help you?"

"My name is John. I'm just ridin' through on my way to Laredo. I wonder if I the owner would let me buy my supper here?"

"I recon he will. This is my ranch. I'm Joseph Cotulla." The man was short of stature though taller than Crudder. He had an accent that John thought was Polish. The man extended his hand.

John shook his hand and said, "I'm John Crudder from Bandera."

"Bandera? Do you know Slim Hanson?" asked Joe.

"Yup. He's my father-in-law."

"Well then, I'm sorry but you can't buy your supper here," said Joe. "But since you're Slim's son-in-law, you will please help yourself to all you can eat."

John followed Joe and the rest of the cowboys into a dining hall that looked remarkably like the one on the H&F. After filling his plate with steak, fried potatoes, and cornbread, John took a seat beside Joe. John found the food to be as good as what was served on the H&F.

Cotulla was easy to talk to and delighted in telling his story of emigrating from Poland and eventually starting his ranch. John listened intently so he didn't miss a word due to Cotulla's accent. Cotulla told him that someday the railroad would run right through the middle of his ranch and take his cattle to market for him without him having to organize trail drives. He also told him there would be a town there and people would want to move there because it was the best place on earth to live.

"How did you get to know Slim?" asked John.

"We met in Brownsville after the war," replied Joe. "I fought for the Union Army and Slim fought for the Confederates. That was a problem for only about five minutes. After that, we realized we both had the dream of owning large cattle ranches but we didn't have much money. Slim had already started the H&F and was helpful to me in showing me how to start a ranch. We decided to work together to see if could make more progress together."

"What did you do to make money?"

"We had a little money and knew we could buy a few head of cattle but it was not nearly enough to make a start toward even one ranch." Joe paused and took another big bite of steak. As he chewed he continued the story. "We went down into Mexico and bought our cattle there. The prices were a lot less than in Texas. Then we drove the cattle all the way to Kansas City and sold them. We made more money than we even dreamed of. Slim had already settled down in Bandera and I came back with intention of going back to Brownsville. This is as far as I got. I fell in love with the land and decided this is where I'd build my ranch."

"From the looks of it, you've done well," said John.

"Yes, I have. I even got up to Slim's ranch a few years ago. I was in San Anton and decided I wanted to see where he settled down. Slim has built a fine ranch." Joe lifted both arms and pointed with his knife and fork to the room. "You might even think you were back on the H&F when you sit in this room."

"I immediately noticed the similarity to the H&F. I thought it was just coincidence."

"No. I liked what Slim had built and decided this would work well on my ranch."

Joe and John continued to visit through the rest of their meal. The cook yelled out, "Apple cobbler!" A loud cheer went up from the men as they descended at once on the cook.

"My cook is named Mo. He's the most popular man on the ranch. After eating his cooking, you can see why. But just wait 'til you've had his apple cobbler." Joe and John continued to talk above the commotion. When the hands were all satisfied, the cook brought two bowls of cobbler over to both men. As with the rest of the meal, it was delicious.

When John finished his cobbler, he went back and got two more bowls and set one in front of Joe. They continued talking as John finished his second bowl of cobbler. As the conversation continued, Joe pushed his bowl in front of John indicating he wasn't going to eat it. As Joe talked on, John finished his third bowl of cobbler.

"John, you're welcomed to bed down in the bunkhouse. In fact, if you would like to stay a few days, feel free to do so. You'll be my guest."

"Thank you, Joe. I'll take you up on the bunkhouse for tonight but I have business in Laredo that will not keep."

"I understand, John. At least stay for breakfast in the morning."

"I certainly will."

* * *

After breakfast, John continued his journey south. Joe told him Encinal was a bit less than thirty miles. John rode through the day and made it to Encinal in early afternoon but didn't stop. He continued to head south, eager to get to Laredo. At dusk, John swung down as he came alongside a small lake. He made camp, brushed Midnight and allowed his horse to drink and graze at will.

That night, John slept well after a dinner consisting of bacon and coffee. As he leaned into his upturned saddle, he marveled that his trip had gone so well. He was expecting to eat bacon at each meal and to sleep under the stars each night. As it turned out, he had fine meals each day and a bed all but one night. He figured he should be in Laredo shortly after noon the next day.

Things would surely take a turn then. He expected to spend his time tracking Marie's killer. While he didn't know what danger he faced he was sure it would require his best. Little did he know Laredo could turn out to be the end of the road for the Midnight Marauder.

Roy Clinton

CHAPTER 10

LAREDO, TEXAS

As John made way into Laredo, he wasn't sure what he was expecting but he found it to be a larger city than he had imagined. He saw some similarities to Bandera and that made him feel very much at home. Immediately he noticed most of the residents were dark-skinned and spoke in Spanish more than English.

It seems Laredo had a push, pull relationship with the United States and Mexico almost since its inception. Laredo was capital of the independent Republic of the Rio Grande in 1840. It was set up in opposition to the Mexican General Antonio Lopez de Santa Anna and effectively became its own country. But such a tiny country could not survive with the great nations to the north and the south. Less than a year after declaring itself a republic, Mexico brought Laredo back by military force. But then after the Mexican-American War in 1846, the town was once again made a part of the United States.

Regardless of the country that claimed it, Laredo was populated mostly by Tejanos, which is Spanish for Mexican-American residents of Texas. That is, they were of Mexican decent and had lived in Laredo for generations. Because of their heritage, they wanted the town to be part of Mexico. The citizens of Laredo got up a petition to ask the American military to return the town to Mexico. The petition was soundly rejected. In response, most of the population moved across the Rio Grande and founded the town of Nuevo Laredo.

John continued through Laredo riding down San Augustin Avenue until he got to the cathedral by the same name. Across the street from the church was a central square that was just a few yards from the Rio Grande River. John looked across the river and knew he was seeing Mexico for the first time. There were a few men milling around the central square. But he saw several men sleeping in the shade of the oak trees that surrounded the square. He knew of the Mexican practice of taking a siesta after lunch. He had seen some of the Mexican hands on the H&F Ranch taking a siesta while the rest of the hands ate. The men on the H&F poked fun at those taking siestas and said they were just not cut out for hard work. But John had observed that the hands of Mexican descent worked just as hard if not harder than the men who had grown up in Bandera.

Swinging down from Midnight, John tied his horse at the hitching rail, removed his hat and walked into the church. He was captivated by the soring ceiling that was arched from one end to the other. The altar at the end of the cathedral was made of white marble and was carved in intricate detail. He slowly walked through the church as he took in the beauty of the building. John walked to the altar and stood for a few minutes and then took a seat in one of the pews, knelt and bowed his head.

Lord, I'm not sure what I'm doing here or why I'm even talking to you. But I get the feeling I'm really going to need your help in the next few days. You know I'm not the superstitious type. Yet I find myself thinking something is going to happen that may be beyond what I can handle. Anyway, whatever is waiting for me, I ask that you will watch over me. Let me make it back home to my wife and daughters.

As John got up from his pew, an elderly priest walked down the aisle. His back was crooked and he was stooped deeply. The priest had a deeply lined face that was dark brown. John realized that the robe the priest was wearing was once white but had taken on a tinge of orange from the red dirt that was held aloft when the wind blew. He carried a tall staff that he used to steady his movements. John held his hat in his hands and greeted him.

"Howdy, Padre."

"Buenos tardes mi hijo."

"I'm sorry, Father, but I don't understand Spanish."

"I just said 'good afternoon, my son.' I don't believe I have seen you in church before. Do you live in Laredo?"

"No, Father. I live in Bandera. I'm here looking for someone."

"If you are looking in church," said the old parson, "he must be a very good man."

"No, he's not," replied John. "I wasn't intending to find him here. I just saw the church and thought I would come inside. It was just an impulse. I'm not sure why I'm even here."

"It looked to me like you were praying."

John paused, looked at the hat he was rolling in his hands. "I guess I was, Father. I do that from time to time but I don't often get into a church to do it."

"My son, it seems like something is troubling you. Would you like to talk about it?"

John sat back down in the pew and the elderly priest sat beside him. Dropping his hat onto the pew, John looked up at the altar and contemplated what he was going to say. He turned his head to the side and took in the beauty of the stained-glass windows. Patiently the old man waited until John was ready to talk.

"Well, Padre, the man I'm looking for, is not a good man at all. He murdered a woman right here in Laredo a few weeks ago."

"What is the woman's name? Perhaps I know her."

"Her name was Marie Hanson."

The old man's eyes sparkled and spoke with excitement. "Consuelo Marie de Zavala Morales Hanson! Si, señor, I knew her very well. She and little Richie were here for mass every week. They never missed. Not once. She was well thought of by everyone in Laredo."

"I just met Richie a few days ago," said John. "He is my brother-in-law. I'm here to find the man who murdered his mother."

"And what are you going to do when you find him?"

"That's what I don't know, Father. I've dealt with bad men

before. Many times."

"Are you a lawman, my son?"

"No, Father. I used to be but I'm not one anymore."

"When you say you've dealt with bad men in the past, what did you mean?"

"Father, I've had to kill men. In fact, I've even killed some women."

The old man drew back in shock at what he was hearing. John saw his surprise and quickly added more.

"It's not like that, Padre. I'm not a bad man. At least I don't think I am. I first killed some cattle rustlers who were trying to kill me and the other hands that worked on the ranch. One of the people they were trying to kill was Richie's father."

"Ah, Señor Hanson. I've never met him."

"That's because he never knew about Richie. Marie left Slim—that's Richie's father—and said she didn't want to see him again. Slim didn't even know about Richie."

"That explains it. Marie never had any unkind words to say about Richie's father. I asked about him and she would only give a vague answer. It was obvious she didn't want to talk about him."

"But Señor, you said you have killed others?"

"Yes, Padre. I was the marshal of Bandera and had to kill some people in the line of duty. I found out the town council were all thieves and murderers and they were able to operate without anyone being able to stop them because they had accomplices in the state police and the governor's office."

"So what did you do, my son?"

"Father, I took the law into my own hands. I thought the only way there would ever be justice in Bandera was if I operated outside of the law to get rid of the town council."

"So you became a vigilante? Is that what you're saying?"

"Yes, Father. I'm not proud of what I've done but I would do it all over again because I didn't see any other way of protecting the people of Bandera. They even kidnapped my wife, Charlotte. She's Slim's daughter so that makes her Richie's half-sister."

"¡Dios no lo quiera!"

"What did you say?"

"I'm sorry. I said, 'God forbid!'"

"Father, I never wanted to kill these people. At least, I didn't start out with that in mind. Before it was over, I had killed many people. All of them deserved it. And if there had been any other way of handling it, I would have welcomed it. But I just didn't see any other way. And after they kidnapped Charlotte, I knew I was going to see that they all paid for what they had done."

The old priest dropped his head and shook it slowly from side to side. In a few moments, he spoke softly.

"I remember hearing of a big man called the Midnight Marauder. He was said to be the defender of those who could not defend themselves. Is…that…?" The old man couldn't complete his sentence. Slowly John nodded his head.

The elderly priest crossed himself and mumbled a hushed prayer in Spanish and then looked into John's eyes.

"You are not such a big man, señor. I mean no offense. But you don't look like the desperado I've heard so much about."

"I guess people just wanted to believe the Midnight Marauder was a large, imposing character. That made their stories of his exploits more sensational. I was glad no one had a more accurate description of me."

"Yes, it would make the stories better to say some huge man had done the things you are said to have done."

"Father," said John. "I've done many bad things but I have not done nearly all of the things I have heard the Midnight Marauder did."

The old man nodded his head. "And what are you going to do if you find the man who murdered Marie?"

"Father, my intention is to bring him in so he can stand trial and then pay for his crime."

"You are not going to take justice into your own hands?"

"That is not my plan. I want to bring him in so others can know what he did and see that he pays for murdering Marie."

The old man's face brightened. One side of his mouth turned up in the tiniest of a smile.

"I'm glad to hear that my son. Then vaya con Dios, my son. Go with God."

"Thank you, Padre."

"What is your name, my son?"

"I'm John Crudder, Father."

"Vaya con Dios, Mr. Crudder. And may the Midnight Marauder never have to accompany you again!"

"That would be just fine with me, Padre."

John walked out of the church, put on his hat and mounted

Midnight. As he proceeded down the road, John felt less anxiety than he had previously. Still he didn't know what he would face but he heard his words to Charlotte come back to him that he was going to be careful. He hoped with all his heart that would be enough to keep him safe.

CHAPTER 11

J ust across from the town square, John found the sheriff's office. He led Midnight over to the hitching rail and went inside.

The sheriff looked up from his desk and said, "Buenas tardes, señor."

"Afternoon, sheriff."

"What can I do for you, young man?" The sheriff looked John up and down and seemed to have a bit of a smile on his face. John was used to people being amused by his small stature.

"I'm here looking for a man."

"What's this man's name?"

"Holloway. Jasper Holloway."

"If you're a bounty hunter, you're wasting your time. Holloway is probably deep into Mexico by now. No one will ever see him again."

"I'm not a bounty hunter."

"You a lawman?" asked the sheriff.

"Used to be. Name's Crudder. John Crudder. I used to be the marshal of Bandera, Texas."

The sheriff pushed his hat back on his head, stood and extended a hand to John. "Pleased to meet you, marshal. I'm JD Lasiter. Just call me JD."

"It's good to meet you, JD. Call me John. And I'm not a marshal any more. Just a private citizen. What's the JD stand for?"

"Nothin'. That's my name. Just JD. Named for my grandpa. He didn't have any other name either. Just JD." John nodded as he took in the name. "So why are you looking for Holloway, John?"

"He killed my brother-in-law's mother."

"You mean Richie Hanson is your brother-in-law?"

"That's right. My wife, Charlotte is Richie's sister."

"I didn't know Richie had a sister."

"Well, it was a surprise to us as well," said John. "We didn't know about Richie until a few days ago when he came riding into Bandera. It seems his mother told him if anything ever happened to her that he was to come to Bandera because he had family there."

"That explains why we haven't seen Richie. I was afraid something had happened to him. He was so angry when Marie got killed. I was sure he was gonna try to take the law into his own hands. He's just a kid. I knew if he tried to go after Holloway, he would wind up dead."

"He has agreed to let me find Holloway for him," said John. "Richie told me you had a poster on Holloway. Mind if I see it?"

"Sure thing, John. I didn't even know we had a poster on Holloway until Richie told us what happened. I was sure sorry to hear about Marie. We all cared deeply for her. She had made several dresses for my wife and my daughter. She was a fine woman. When Richie told us what happened, I had Marie's body taken to the undertaker and helped Richie arrange for her funeral. I also swore out murder charges on Holloway. He was also wanted for cattle rustlin', horse theft, and assaulting a man in San Anton."

John looked over the wanted poster. Knowing Holloway had been to San Antonio made John optimistic that he had gone north instead of south.

"Do you mind if I go through the rest of your posters, sheriff."

"Not at all, John." The sheriff opened the bottom drawer to his desk and pulled out a stack of papers that was several inches thick and handed them to John. Crudder sat down on the other side of the desk and started sorting through the posters. "You being an ex-lawman and all, I don't mind a bit. Now I wouldn't be lettin' you do so if I thought you were a bounty hunter and was just plannin' to start lookin' for any outlaw. If you don't mind me askin', what are you lookin' for?"

"Tell you the truth, I don't know. I just remember back when I was a marshal, sometimes going through the posters would give me some ideas and even give me a clue on where to find someone. Like Holloway here. You said he was probably in Mexico now. But I'm thinkin' it might be more likely he was headed back to San Anton since that is where I know he's been before. Of course, he could just want to get as far away from San Anton and now Laredo as possible, so he certainly could be headed into the interior of Mexico."

"Well, you take your time. The only thing I ask is that you not take any of the posters. I only have the one copy so I need to keep them."

"I understand, JD. I'll not need to take any with me. If there is anything interesting, I'll just make some notes to myself."

As John started through the stack of posters, he found a drawing of a man that looked identical to Holloway, only the name on the poster said Martinez.

"Look at this, sheriff. Diego Martinez is a spittin' image of Holloway."

"Do you reckon that's his brother?" asked the sheriff.

"No, JD. I think that is Holloway. Or I think Holloway is Martinez. An easy way to escape a wanted poster is to use a different name and to get away from the city where the crime had been committed. It makes me wonder if there are any other posters on Diego Martinez."

"Give me half," said the sheriff. "I'll go through them with you."

For the next thirty minutes, John and the sheriff sorted through posters. They found several for Diego Martinez that didn't have a picture but had descriptions that fit Holloway.

"Hey John. Look at this one."

The sheriff passed John a poster with a drawing that was nearly identical to Martinez and Holloway. But this time, the name on the poster was Luis Hernandez. The continued through the posters and made stacks of posters or all three names. Then they had one more stack that had descriptions that fit Holloway. They had a variety of names including Smith and Jones. But all of the posters were for violent crimes including several for murder and rape. Several of the posters were for bank robbery. There were people killed in two of the holdups.

By the time they were through sorting, they had more than a dozen posters that John was sure fit Holloway and more than twenty additional posters that could be Holloway. All of the posters were for crimes committed in Texas with several committed in Austin and San Antonio and in many of the small towns around in the Texas Hill Country. John was more convinced than ever that Holloway was still in Texas.

"JD, do you know if Holloway spoke Spanish?"

The sheriff, thought for a minute and said, "I don't know if I ever heard him speak Spanish but almost everyone in Laredo does. But it's not like he grew up here. He had only been in town for a few months. From all accounts, he was just a drifter that spent most of his time at the Bustin' Loose Saloon."

"Several of the posters list known associates of Holloway. And assuming Martinez, and Hernandez are also Holloway, we have their associates as well. It seems there are two men that hung around with Holloway." John continued perusing the posters. "Gomez and Atkins were in on several of the crimes. They don't have first names listed. But the descriptions of both men fit that of the men with Holloway on the bank robberies. Have you seen either of these men in town?"

"I had no idea Holloway was wanted for so many crimes. And he was right here under my nose for months."

"Sheriff, the important thing now is not to lay blame for not knowing but to do all we can to find him."

"John, I really don't know what else I can do. I can't go hunt him down. I have a city to protect. As much as I'd like to organize and lead a posse, I have responsibilities here."

"I realize that, Sheriff. Actually, I think a posse would just drive Holloway to ground. I think he will be easier to find if I go by myself."

"You're probably right. But it will likely take time. I'm sure you know that from your law enforcement background."

John pondered what the sheriff said. "Yup. I reckon it might take a while. But I'm a patient man. I'll take all of the time required to find Holloway. And findin' him, I think I'll find Martinez and Hernandez."

"If you are going to do that, I'd like to deputize you. You might find a badge will help open some doors for you."

"Thanks, Sheriff. But if it's all the same to you, I think I will do better without the badge."

Sheriff Lasiter looked at John and considered what he said. Slowly a smile came to the sheriff's face and he slightly nodded his head. "Yes, you just may do better without a badge. Just remember, all three men are wanted and need to be brought back here for trial. At least let me give you a pair of handcuffs. I can only spare one pair but I think that should help."

"Thanks, Sheriff. What I can tell you is Holloway will pay for what he's done. I'll bring him back here to stand trial if I can. And I'll bring his compadres with him. I would like nothin' more than to see them punished for their crimes."

The sheriff was not convinced by John's words. He continued staring at Crudder trying to figure out what was going on his mind. Finally, the sheriff put out his hand to wish John well.

"Mr. Crudder, I hope you're successful in finding Holloway. But be careful. It seems Holloway is a lot more dangerous than I ever realized."

"Thanks, Sheriff." John shook hands with Lasiter and turned to go. But as he got to the door he turned back. "Sheriff, who in town would have more information about Holloway?"

"Well, I guess Manny could tell you more about Holloway. He runs the Bustin' Loose just down the street. Holloway appears to have spent most of his time there."

"Thanks again, Sheriff." John left the sheriff's office and walked out to Midnight. "We'll be goin' real soon ol boy. I have one more errand to run." Midnight whinnied in response. John smiled to himself as he petted his horse on the rump and walked down to the saloon.

John walked up to the bar and ordered a beer. The barkeeper filled his glass and expertly slid it down to John. Behind him, John heard laughter from men who were playing poker.

"Hey boys. Look at the size of this guy." The speaker laughed out loud and continued to taunt John. "He can barely see over the bar. Hey, sonny, would you like for me to get you a stool to stand on?" John looked back at the man and saw there were three of them and they were all laughing loudly.

"Thanks just the same, mister," replied John. "So long as I can see enough to get my beer, that's all I need." John turned back to his beer but quickly located the table in the mirror behind the bar.

"Hey, Sonny. Don't turn your back on me, you little runt." With those words the loud talking gambler lunged at John. John stepped to the side and grabbed the shirt of the man and slammed him into the bar. As the man was regaining his balance, John brought his fist up under the man's chin and connected with a single blow. The attacker instantly fell to the floor. At the same time, the remaining two gamblers got up and pulled their six-guns and aimed at John.

John lifted his hands high above his head as though he was trying to stop them men from shooting him. Then in one movement, Crudder dropped his hands down his back and grabbed the twin daggers that were just under his vest, dropped to his knee, and let both daggers go, simultaneously hitting both men in the chest. The men dropped to the floor as the first gambler came to and pulled his gun on John. Crudder rolled away from the gunman and pulled his own six-gun with his right hand and fanned the hammer once with his left hand. John's bullet hit the gunman in the middle of the chest.

John slowly got to his feet and kept his gun out trained on the man he had just shot. He also turned to see if the men he had taken down with his daggers had moved but saw they were dead. Holstering his gun, John walked back to the bar and took a swallow of his beer as he saw the sheriff barging in through the swinging doors with his gun cocked and ready to fire.

"What's goin' on here?" yelled the sheriff.

John took another swallow of his beer as the bartender replied to the sheriff.

"Sheriff Lasiter, it was the darndest thing I've ever seen. This little feller took out all three of these drifters and they had it comin'. He was just standin' here drinkin' his beer when this first feller attacked him. The little man just stepped aside and hit him once under the chin and the man dropped to the floor. Then his two friends got up and drew down on the little feller. But he pulled them knives from his back and killed 'em both. Then this guy," continued the bartender as he pointed down at the dead man by the bar, "pulled his gun on the little feller. The little guy rolled and somehow came up with his own gun and shot this here man dead. And the little feller was in the right. He didn't have no choice."

A man who was standing at the other end of the bar spoke up. "That's right, Sheriff. It's just as Manny said. The little man didn't have no choice at all. He was in the right."

The sheriff carefully uncocked and holstered his gun and walked over to Crudder. "May I buy you a beer, Sheriff?" asked John.

"Well, Mr. Crudder, I was worried about you when you left my office. I thought you might get in over your head if you were ever in a gunfight. But I can see I don't need to worry about you. Yes, I could use a beer."

The bartender poured the sheriff's beer and asked John if he would like his glass topped off.

"No, thanks. But you can help me if you will. My name is John Crudder. I'm lookin' for a man named Jasper Holloway. The sheriff said you might be able to help me."

The barkeeper extended his hand to John and said, "I'm pleased to meet you Mr. Crudder. My name's Manny. I've never seen anything like what you just did to those men."

John shook the offered hand and said, "Manny, what can you tell me about Holloway?"

"Well, we all called him Percy. Didn't know his name was really Jasper 'til you told me. Percy was here might near every day drinkin' and playin' poker. He was always gettin' into fights. And he always won. I never did like him none. He was a no-account drifter that was just a troublemaker. I asked him to leave several times but he made it clear he was gonna stay as long as he wanted and if I tried to get him to leave before he was ready, he'd hurt me. I just tried to leave him be. I didn't want no trouble."

"Where there any men that hung around with Holloway?" asked John.

"There was a man named Gomez and another named Atkins that were usually with him. They would play poker with Holloway but mostly they just drank and carried on with the ladies that work here."

"What did Gomez and Atkins look like?" asked Crudder.

"Both men were around medium height. They had dark skin and looked mean. Gomez always wore a tan shirt and had a black hat that had a hatband made of silver pesos. Atkins had a limp when he walked. I heard him say he was thrown by a horse once and it messed up his knee."

"Any idea where they might have headed after leavin Laredo?" asked John.

Manny stopped and considered the question. "I know they have worked on ranches before. One of the men, I think it was Atkins, said they had worked on the Cotulla Ranch. It's between Encinal and Frio City. But I also heard 'em talk about ranches around San Anton. Seems like they talked about which ranches but I don't recall the names."

"I was just on the Cotulla Ranch a few days ago. I know exactly where it is." John turned and spoke to the sheriff. "Sheriff, more than ever, I think Holloway is headed back north. He could've gone to Mexico but it seems more likely he will be goin' back to the places he knows best."

The sheriff nodded in agreement. "I think you're right. I would have guessed he would have headed to Mexico to try to get lost. But I'm inclined to agree that he is probably still in Texas."

John placed a silver dollar on the bar and thanked Manny for his information. John started to walk out the door but then looked down at the three bodies on the floor. He went over and withdrew his daggers from the bodies, cleaned them on the dead men's shirts and reinserted them into the double scabbard on his back. "Sheriff, here's ten dollars to help pay for burying these men. The undertaker shouldn't have to work for free."

"Thanks, John. I hope you catch Holloway and the others. And if you can, bring them back here to stand trial."

"That's my plan. I just hope they'll allow me to do that."

Crudder walked out of the saloon, untied Midnight, swung up, and headed north down San Augustin Avenue. He didn't know where his travels would take him but he was confident he would find Holloway.

Roy Clinton

CHAPTER 12

BANDERA, TEXAS

D addy, I think today is the day for me to get some furniture for Richie's room. Would you mind watching the girls while I go to town?" Charlotte was holding both daughters by their hands.

"Of course, I don't mind," replied Slim. "Come here, girls. You get to play with grandpa this morning." Both girls broke free from their mother's grasp and ran toward Slim. He bent down and gathered them in his arms and twirled them around the living room. "We're gonna have a great time, aren't we, girls?" The twins just laughed as a reply.

"Where's Richie? I would like for him to go with me. I don't want to pick out things that he might not like?"

"He's out in the barn. I let him pick out a new horse," replied Slim. "He has been brushin' him so much, I'll bet he's gonna brush that poor horse bald."

Charlotte laughed at the comment and bounded down the steps

of the porch on her way to the barn. Inside, she found Richie was indeed brushing his horse and talking softly to the stud. He was a buckskin that was golden brown with a dark brown mane and tail and tall brown socks. "He sure is handsome. What are you going to name him?"

"I don't know. I haven't thought about it 'til you brought it up. What do you think I should name him?"

"Richie, he's your horse. It's up to you to decide what you want to name him." Richie continued his brushing and had a pensive look. Deep in thought, he was silent for several minutes except for some whispering to his horse.

"I know what I'll call him. I want to call him Laredo. When I call his name, it'll always remind me of where I grew up."

"That sounds fine, Richie. I like that." Richie continued brushing his horse and whispering and asking if he liked his new name.

"I'm headed to town to get you some furniture for your room. Will you go with me and pick out what you would like?"

"Yes, ma'am. I sure will," replied Richie.

"Richie Hanson. I'm your sister. You don't have to call me ma'am."

"I'm sorry Charlotte. It's just that Ma always taught me to say ma'am to women. It's just a habit."

"Come to think of it," Charlotte said, "I think it's a fine habit. Your mother raised you well. It's important for a young man to have good manners. If you want to call me ma'am, that's fine with me. So will you hitch up the wagon? If we find some furniture we like, we can bring it home. Otherwise, we'll have to order it and have it delivered."

"Yes, ma'am, I will."

Charlotte smiled as she watched Richie hurriedly gather the team from the corral and get them into their harnesses. He expertly hitched both horses to the wagon and then helped Charlotte onto the wagon seat. Sitting down beside her, he gently popped the reins and the horses moved into a slow trot as they left the barn and headed to town. As they made their way toward Bandera, Charlotte continued to learn more about her brother.

"Richie," Charlotte asked, "How far did you get in school?"

"I graduated last summer. The school was right across the street from our house. I loved school so my teacher let me move ahead at my own pace. I graduated a whole year early."

"What are you planning on doing now?"

"Don't really know. I haven't given it much thought lately. My thoughts have all been about losing Ma. I can't imagine what the future will be without her. She has always been there for me."

Charlotte laid her hand on Richie's knee. "I know a little of what you're talking about. I miss my mother, too, but I never got to know her. She died when I was a baby. Richie, have you ever thought about going to college?"

"Yes. I was supposed to be there now. I got an academic scholarship to Baylor University in Independence. I was taking off for one semester to work and make some money to help Ma out. Since Ma got killed, I haven't even thought about going to college."

"Richie, this is your life and this is your time. You need to go to college. It would be a shame not to continue your education. You have such great potential. College will help you explore what you want to do with your life. As smart as you are, I know you can literally do anything you want to do."

"Thank you, Charlotte, I know you're right. But for now, I want to stay on the ranch with you, Pa, and John and the twins. This is more family that I've ever had. I just don't want to leave you now, especially after just losing Ma."

"That's understandable, Richie. But promise me you'll start when the time is right."

Richie chewed his lip as he contemplated Charlotte's request. He knew she was right he needed to continue his education. "All right, Charlotte. I'll start in the fall."

"What had you planned to study at Baylor?"

"I know this probably doesn't sound like such a great idea. But I wanted to study law and become a lawyer."

Charlotte chuckled a bit as she thought about Richie's words.

"I hope you're not making fun of me, Charlotte."

"I'm sorry, Richie. Of course I'm not making fun of you. I was just thinking not only is my husband a lawyer but now I find I have a brother and he wants to be a lawyer too."

"John's a lawyer?" asked Richie.

"He certainly is. When he finished law school, he planned to come to Bandera and open a law practice. But he soon realized he needed to be in a bigger city if he was going to have a practice large enough to keep him busy."

"Where did he go to law school?"

"He went to Harvard. Actually, John's got two degrees from Harvard and one from Oxford in England."

"Wow! I didn't have any idea he had that kind of education. I guess you never know what a person's background is. Do you think he will ever open a law practice?"

Charlotte giggled and said, "I've learned with John, there's no telling what he'll do next. I know he was in New York a few months ago and he was in court several times dealing with some business there."

"Really? I've never met anyone who's been to New York. Have you ever been there, Charlotte?"

"No, I haven't. But John grew up there. I'm sure when he gets home he will be glad to tell you all about it."

"That would be nice. I would like to go to New York someday." Richie had a bit of a smile on his face as he contemplated making a future trip to east. There was little doubt in his mind he would do that.

When they left for town, Charlotte directed Richie to take the wagon over to the general store. Inside they found the proprietor had just gotten in a new shipment of furniture.

"Mr. Anderson, I would like for you to meet Richie. Richie, this is Mr. Anderson."

Richie removed his hat and extended his hand. "Pleased to meet you Mr. Anderson."

"And I'm pleased to meet you young man. Charlotte, your friend certainly does have good manners."

"Yes, he does, Mr. Anderson. And Richie is going to be staying on the H&F with us so we need to get him some furniture."

"Very good. What did you have in mind?"

"Well, I think he needs a bed and a chest of drawers. He also needs an armoire and probably a desk and a chair. Oh yes, he needs a table to put beside his bed. An easy chair would be nice. What do you think, Richie?"

Richie was completely overwhelmed by Charlotte's generosity. He didn't know what to say so he just said, "I guess that sounds fine."

Charlotte walked through the furniture and helped Richie select the pieces he needed. For the most part her selections met with his approval. She found an armoire that captured her attention. "Oh Richie, look at this. Isn't it darling?"

The piece was sitting on fancy carved legs and had decorative carving above the door. It was painted in a pale yellow. Richie looked at it and tried not to react. Mr. Anderson quickly realized the piece didn't appeal to Richie.

"Charlotte," said Mr. Anderson, "Don't you think that is a bit feminine for such a masculine young man?"

Charlotte laughed out loud. "You're absolutely right, Mr. Anderson. I'm sorry Richie. For a minute I forgot we were shopping for you. I was thinking how beautiful that would be in my bedroom. Mr. Anderson, help us select some masculine furniture that will be to the liking of my friend."

For the next half of an hour, the three of them walked through the store and made selections. To Charlotte's delight, they found all of the furniture they needed in stock in the store, relieving them of having to place a special order. "Mr. Anderson, we need to go down to the hardware store to buy some paint. Do you have anyone who can load the furniture onto our wagon?"

"Yes, I do, Charlotte. You go ahead and get your paint. I'll have it loaded by the time you get back."

Charlotte and Richie walked down the street and entered the hardware store. They looked at several colors of paint. This time Richie didn't hesitate to express his opinion. He convinced Charlotte the pale blue paint she adored was not something he cared for—and it was the same for the yellow and the pink that was called rose.

He selected a dark beige paint saying he thought it would look good with the new furniture. Charlotte agreed and asked the storekeeper to put the paint on their bill. They walked back to the wagon and found Mr. Anderson's workers were just completing tying the furniture securely to the wagon.

"Thank you, Mr. Anderson. I am so pleased with our purchases."

"You're welcome, Charlotte. I'm glad you like your selections. I think the furniture will last for many years. And Richie, it was good to meet you. I hope I get to see you again."

Richie helped Charlotte into the wagon and then climbed up beside her. As they headed back to the H&F, Richie turned to her and asked, "Why didn't you tell him I was your brother?"

"Well, Richie, I was going to. But then I realized everyone in town would soon have heard the news. I think Daddy needs to be the one who shares the news. It is up to him who he tells and what he wants to say."

"That makes sense, Sis. I didn't think about that." Charlotte giggled again. "What's so funny?"

"You called me Sis. I like that."

Richie laughed back at Charlotte. "I didn't even realize I had done that until you mentioned it. I kind of like the sound of it too. I've never had a sister before."

Arriving at the ranch, Charlotte asked Richie to pull the wagon into the barn and leave the furniture loaded. "I want to get your room painted before we unload the wagon."

Charlotte wasted no time in getting two ranch hands to help clear the existing furniture out of Richie's room and put drop cloths down on the floor. To their horror, when they finished moving the furniture, she handed each a paintbrush.

"Gentlemen, thank you so much for helping me paint Richie's room. It will not take long with four of us painting."

"But Miss Charlotte," one of the men complained, "we have work to do." Then the other man said, "Owen and Slim will expect us to have it done by this evening. We would like to help you paint but we just don't have time."

"Well good. Since you would like to help, I'll be sure to tell Daddy that you had an important job to do for me. I know it will be all right with him." Both men let out partially concealed groans. They realized it was pointless to argue with Charlotte once she had her mind made up. Each of them took a brush and dipped it in the paint. When Richie had tended to the team, he came in to find

Charlotte had a brush waiting for him. "Richie, these men have volunteered to help us paint your room. Hurry and get your brush going. With four of us, we will be through in no time."

The two conscripted cowboys exchanged a glance and then looked at Richie, who just rolled his shoulders and dipped his brush in the paint. Less than an hour later, Charlotte backed up and inspected their work. "Gentlemen, you did a marvelous job. Thank you so much for your help. Richie, you take the brushes and get them soaking in turpentine. These men will help me move your furniture in."

"Miss Charlotte, we would like to but we have to get back to our ranch chores."

"Don't you worry about it. It will only take you a few minutes to bring the furniture in. And when you bring it in, remember the walls are still wet. We don't want to have to repaint them, do we?"

"No ma'am," said the cowboys in unison."

It didn't take very long before all the furniture was in place. Charlotte offered to get the men some coffee but they declined and rapidly left the house. It was clear they were glad to have escaped before Charlotte found more work for them to do.

Roy Clinton

CHAPTER 13

ENCINAL, TEXAS

C rudder held Midnight back to a gentle lope as he rode out of Laredo. He rode for about fifteen miles before he camped for the night. He took Midnight well off the road winding through the blackbrush, brasil, and other thorny plants. Cactus was plentiful and seemed to grow everywhere. There was a tiny lake just off the road with a small grove of mesquite trees on the bank. John unsaddled Midnight and built a fire. He then pulled the dandy brush from his saddlebag and gave Midnight a good brushing. When Midnight saw the brush, he let out a low, guttural nicker and nodded his head up and down.

John laughed at his horse and realized the majestic animal knew he was going to be groomed. For much of the next hour, John brushed Midnight and combed his main and tail. With his horse cared for, John turned his attention to supper. He cut a hunk of bacon from the slab and threaded it on a stick. Propping the stick up so it was over the fire, John made a pot of coffee and put it on a flat stone near the fire. He wished he had something more to eat but knew the bacon and coffee would sustain him until he had more.

That evening, John slept soundly as Midnight grazed nearby. Just before sunrise, John woke up and warmed up his left-over coffee. At first light, he had Midnight saddled and then continued on toward Encinal. He guessed it was about twenty-five miles away.

About noon, John spotted a jackrabbit. He pulled his saddle gun and quickly dispatched the little animal. Swinging down, he skinned and dressed the rabbit. After building a fire, John roasted the rabbit and then wasted no time in devouring every bit. It was a bit gamey but John liked it because it was something different from the bacon that was his mainstay when he was on the trail.

After eating, he continued on and got to Encinal by late afternoon. The town had only a small general store, a livery stable, and a saloon that doubled as a café. He took Midnight to the livery and groomed him. He paid for a bucket of oats and asked the old man who was tending the stable to have him saddled by first light the next day.

"I'm lookin' for a man. Maybe you've seen him. His name is Holloway. His given name is Jasper but he also goes by Percy."

"Friend of yours?" asked the stableman.

"No. He's a murderer. I'm looking to take him back to Laredo to stand trial."

"What's he look like?"

"He's missing part of his right ear and has a scar that goes from his ear down his cheek. And he has a spider tattooed on the back of his left hand."

"Yup, I saw him. You a lawman?" The old man continued to look suspiciously at John.

"No. Used to be. Now I'm just a rancher. But Holloway murdered my brother-in-law's mother. I'm here to find him and take him back to Laredo to stand trial."

Finally, the stableman decided he could trust John so he opened up about what he knew. "He was here two or three weeks ago. Was riding a flea-bitten grey mare."

"Was he alone?"

"No. Now that you mention it, there were two other men with him. One had a fancy black hat that had a headband made out of silver pesos. The other man walked with a limp. I didn't get their names but the man with the fancy hat was riding a bay. The man with the limp was riding a dun."

"How much do I owe you for the oats and stabling my horse?" asked John.

"Four bits will cover it." John gave him a silver dollar. "I don't have change mister. Don't you have any quarters?"

"The dollar is for my horse and a thank you for the information you gave me. I learned a lot about the men I'm looking for thanks to you."

The old man smiled and put the silver dollar in his pocket. "If I think on it right smart, I may come up with more information."

John smiled at the old man and headed over to the saloon to get something to eat. Inside, he took a table in the corner and soon a waitress came to take his order. "What can I get you, Hon?"

The woman was well past sixty and had a weathered face with deep-set eyes, heavily hooded by her eyelids, giving her a sleepy look. Her long eyelashes peaked out from under her eyelids. Over the next few minutes she told John about the menu ("steak and taters, or only steak"), her "no-account husband" who left her twenty years before, her childhood growing up in San Antonio, and her father who was a peddler of housewares ("he always came home for momma's cooking"). John listened to her discourse until she ran out of steam. It took her all of five minutes to finish her stories and during that time she fowled the air with her colorful language.

"So, Hon, what would you like to eat?"

"I think I'll take the steak and taters. And when you get that ordered, I'd be glad to buy you a beer if you would come back and visit with me."

Her face brightened and she batted her long lashes at John. "Well, cowboy, it's a deal. I'll be right back and I'll even pour my own beer."

She shouted the order through an open window beside the bar, cussing like a sailor as she did. She then filled a mug with beer and went over to John's table. "So what do you have in mind, Hon. I don't get off work until late but I've been told I'm pretty good company."

John cleared his throat and tried to organize his thoughts. "Ma'am, I may have given you the wrong impression. I'm not after companionship. I just need a little bit of information."

The woman's countenance fell for a second but she quickly recovered. "Hey, Cowboy. I knew that. You're younger than my son." She let out a loud laugh and a string of colorful words and then said, "So, what kind of information can 'ol Ruby give you?"

Another waitress brought John's supper. He wasted no time in digging in to his steak. The jackrabbit he had that morning was long gone. But he didn't get more than a couple of bites down before he realized Ruby was going to demand his undivided attention.

"I'm pleased to meet you, Miss Ruby. My name's John. John Crudder."

"Well howdy, John. What can I tell you?"

"A few weeks ago, three men came through here. They were bad men. All of them have a number of wanted posters on them." John spent the next several minutes describing the men and telling Ruby about their past crimes and ending with the account of them murdering Marie Hanson.

She cursed and swore as she heard about the murder of Marie. She had many choice words for the men. "And the man named Holloway; he's rotten as a bad apple. All three of 'em were in here and Holloway got rough with me. He slapped me around. He hit me even harder than that no-account ex-husband of mine did."

John listened to her story and of the venomous words she had for Holloway and his companions. They told her they were working on the Dawson ranch that was just out of town. She gave John directions and then leaned into him and said, "Hon, are you sure you don't want no company later tonight?" Then she leaned back and let out a loud laugh. John left two dollars to pay for his dinner and to tip Ruby and then headed over to the livery stable where he bedded down beside Midnight.

When morning came, John was up before the stableman made it to work. He saddled his horse and headed out east of town to find the Dawson ranch. The directions Ruby had given him the day before were accurate and easy to follow. As Crudder left the main road to head to the ranch, he watched a small herd of deer scurry off and move out of sight. Everywhere John looked, he saw an abundance of mesquite trees and cactus. The soil was light red and sandy. Even though it was early February, the air was hot.

The road ended at the ranch. In front of Crudder stood an arched entrance made of stone. Stone walls extended from the arch for more than one hundred yards in both directions. Clearly this was a large ranch.

John rode through the arch and took the wagon road about a quarter mile. Though Midnight wanted to run, Crudder didn't want to call attention to his presence. Ahead, John saw a large stone house and a corral made of stone. There were two unpainted wooden barns and another structure that looked like it might be a bunkhouse or dining hall.

Crudder swung down and tied Midnight to the hitching rail in front of the bunkhouse. Inside, John discovered the building had no interior walls. Bunks were set up on the perimeter of the room and there were tables in the middle. A few hands were milling around, finishing their meals. John carefully looked at the men but saw none of them fit the description of Holloway or his accomplices. He walked up to one of the men who had just finished his meal.

"Where can I find the foreman?" asked Crudder.

Looking John over carefully, the man pointed to an older gentleman that was lying on a bunk, propped up on pillows, drinking coffee. The man was wearing one boot and had a splint made of thin strips of wood on his other leg.

"Howdy," said John as he removed his hat. "Are you the foreman?"

"I am if you're lookin' for a job." The man took a longer look at John and continued. "My, but you're a little feller. That don't matter none. If you want a job, you got one. Get you somethin' to eat and go outside and look for Claude. He'll get you lined out."

"I thank you kindly for the offer of a job but I'm not lookin' for work. I'm lookin' for somebody."

The old cowboy set down his tin cup and stuck out his hand. "Name's Colby. I'm foreman and until yesterday, I was the hardest workin' cowboy on the Dawson Ranch."

John shook Colby's hand. "Name's John Crudder. What happened to your leg?"

"I got throwed. Ain't no horse never throwed me before yesterday. But some nitwit threw a rattlesnake at my horse. I got throwed and then my own horse stomped me trying to get to the snake."

"That's just mean," said John. "Wasn't he afraid of getting snake bit himself?"

"Nah. Found out later the snake was dead. The blame fool said he was just playin' a little joke and wanted to see what I'd do. Well, I'll tell you what I did. I fired him on the spot. And I fired his two friends who were in on it and were laughing as my horse stomped me."

John's ears immediately perked up. "Was the man's name Holloway?"

"It shor was. How on earth could you have known that?"

"'Cause I'm huntin' Holloway. He murdered the mother of a friend of mine in Laredo a few weeks ago. He usually travels with two men named Gomez and Atkins."

"That's them. All three men are of no-account. If I wasn't so short of hands, I never would have hired 'em."

"How long have they worked here?" asked Crudder.

"Must be nigh onto two months. At first, I was tickled to get three new hands at once. We have more beef than we can care for now. But I soon realized they were lazy and shiftless. They were just looking for a place to stay and grub to eat. It was like they needed a place where they could hide for a while."

"That sounds exactly like what they were doin'," said John. "All three men are wanted for robbin' banks as well as cattle rustlin' and horse theft. There is a string of people who have died as they committed their crimes. You're lucky they're not around here anymore."

"You're right about that," said Colby. "And they could of caused right smart trouble 'round here. All they would have had to do was to take out a few of the hands and then they could have stolen Dawson's whole herd."

"Any idea where they went when they left here?"

"No. And I don't care. So long as they are not around me, I don't care where they went."

"Do you think they kept goin' north or would they've turned back to Laredo?"

"Young feller, I told you I don't know."

"I'm sorry Mr. Colby. I just want to catch 'em before they kill someone else." John clamped his hat back on and said, "Thanks for the information. I'm glad you weren't hurt any worse."

"Crudder, go get you something to eat before you get goin'. There's still some breakfast left. You're not wasting time by eatin'. A body's got to have food."

"Thank you kindly, sir. I'm much obliged." John walked over to what was left of the breakfast and got several spoonfuls of scrambled eggs, bacon, and a couple of biscuits. He pulled the biscuits apart and poured gravy over them. After grabbing a cup of coffee, he took his plate to a nearby table and hurriedly cleaned his plate. When he was through, he went back and filled his plate again.

He hadn't realized how hungry he was. John smiled to himself as he remembered neglecting his supper the night before when Ruby was intent on flirting with him. He felt he escaped a very awkward situation when he left most of his steak and said good-bye to Ruby.

As John was finishing his meal, Colby hobbled on his crutches over to John. "Young feller, you have a powerful appetite. And I've got a feelin' you're a top hand. You do work on a ranch, don't you?"

Swallowing and taking yet another bite, John responded. "Yup. Work on the H&F in Bandera."

"Shor wish you could work here a while. I've taken a likin' to you. After you find Holloway and his bunch, if you want a job, there'll be one waitin' for you."

"Thanks all the same. But my wife and daughters are back on the H&F waitin' for me to get home."

"I never heard of a cowboy having his family livin' on the ranch where he works. How'd that happen? You the foreman or somethin'?"

"No," replied John. "My wife is the daughter of the ranch owner."

The old man doubled over laughing. "Boy, that's a good one. You shor found a way to get in good with the boss. More power to you, son." Colby continued laughing as John completed his meal.

There were times in John's life when he would have taken offense to the old man's words. But he knew Colby meant no harm. And John laughed to himself as he thought of the situation and how close he had grown to Slim, even before marrying his daughter.

John wished Colby well with his leg and went outside and mounted Midnight. As he headed back to the main road, he wondered which way he would turn when he left there. Would he go left and head back into Laredo or turn right and head to the next town? By the time the road he was on met up with El Camino Real, he knew he needed to keep heading north so he turned right and let Midnight run for about fifteen minutes before reining him back to a lope.

He had often wondered about the limit to Midnight's endurance. So far he knew that Midnight had more stamina than any horse he had ever heard of. He recalled once a couple of years before when he had gone from Bandera to San Antonio and back on the same day—a distance of over a hundred miles. And he recalled Midnight was a bit winded but didn't seem to be overly tired.

Even though would like to let Midnight run as much as he wanted, he also knew the mighty horse would be better off to take a more measured pace. Before he found Holloway, John knew he might be calling on Midnight to push his limits. Little did he know that time was fast approaching.

Roy Clinton

CHAPTER 14

COTULLA RANCH

J ohn Crudder continued north heading back down the road he traveled only a few days before. He allowed Midnight to lope most of the way. But every time they passed a stream or a lake, John would stop and let Midnight rest, drink water, and graze for a few minutes.

Toward evening, he neared the Cotulla Ranch and remembered the wonderful meal he had there earlier. John's plan was to stay the night and then keep heading north the next morning. As John got to the ranch, he pulled up in front of the dining hall. Sure enough, it looked like supper was just being served.

John tied Midnight to the hitching rail and went inside. Just inside the door, he heard Cotulla's unmistakable voice.

"John! Johnny boy!" Joseph Cotulla's polish accent was very much in evidence. "What are you doin' back here so soon? No matter. It's time to eat. Get yourself a plate and come join me."

John waved at Cotulla with his hat and walked over to get in line behind the ranch hands. When he got to the head of the line, he found to his surprise, fried chicken was on the menu. He had just assumed with it being a cattle ranch, most of the meals would be steak.

As John held out his plate to get served, the big man who was serving up chicken turned toward John. He was well over six feet tall and had a huge potbelly that was a good advertisement for his cooking. John recalled the cook's name was Mo and Joe saying he was the most popular man on the ranch. Mo was wearing a bright red plaid shirt covered by a dirty white apron.

He spoke to John. "I heard Joe call you Johnny boy. You're the same John that a few days ago came through and ate three helpings of my apple cobbler."

John was embarrassed as he recalled all that he ate that night. "Well, I guess that was me. Sorry I ate so much. I was powerful hungry."

Mo brought his big arm around and slapped John hard on his arm. John's plate went flying. Fortunately, the plate was made of tin so it made noise as it contacted the floor but it did no damage. Mo laughed and patted John twice more on the arm.

"I like to see cowboys eat. No apology needed. I hope you've got a good appetite for fried chicken. I got plenty of it. And I've got mashed taters and green beans. But I'm sorry; got no cobbler tonight. All I've got for dee-sert is 'nana puddin'. You ever had 'nana puddin'?"

"No, sir. Can't say I have. What is it?"

Mo let out a loud laugh at John's question. "Hey boys, young

John here ain't never had 'nana puddin'. Where you been all your life boy? New York City?"

"Well—actually, I have spent most of my life in New York. Only been in Texas a few years."

Mo laughed again. "That explains it. Anyone that's really Texan to the core, knows 'nana puddin' as well as he does apple cobbler."

"All right. You've got me. I'm from New York and I've never had 'nana puddin'. Tell me what's in it. I'm sure I'll like it."

Mo went on to give John a quick recipe. "You cut 'nanas up and put them in a bowl with little sugar wafers. You mix in puddin' made from milk, egg yolks, sugar, and butter. Cook it up, add a little vanilla extract. Pour it all together with the 'nanas and the sugar wafers and keep it in the oven 'til supper is over. I like to serve it hot. That's the best way to eat it."

John picked up his plate and let Mo fill it with chicken and all the fixings, then took his plate over to join Joseph. "Hello, Mr. Cotulla. Thanks kindly for feedin' me again."

"Did you forget. I'm just Joe. Not Mr. Cotulla." John nodded as he attacked a chicken leg. "I see you met Mo." Cotulla laughed at the meeting. "And Mo gave you a ribbin' about not knowing about 'nana puddin'. You are in for a treat tonight."

"Actually, Joe, I didn't know what a 'nana was. Then I realized he was talkin' about bananas. I've been pretty successful at getting New York out of my voice but there are still some things in Texas that I have yet to experience."

"So what brings you back here so soon?" asked Joe.

"I'm lookin' for some men. The leader is a man named Holloway. He's missin' part of his ear and has a spider tattoo on his left hand."

"I'll bet the other men your lookin for are named Gomez and Atkins."

"That's right! You mean they're here?" John was excited that his hunt might be over.

"No, son, they ain't here but they've been here. They was here probably a year ago. They're no good. All three of 'em. I run 'em off 'cause all they did was cause trouble and eat grub. Now I don't mind hands eatin' and eatin' a lot. But I do mind men eatin' who don't work. The Good Book says, 'If any man would not work, neither should he eat.' That's from Second Thessalonians, chapter three, verse ten."

John paused realizing he had a pile of chicken bones in his plate and he was just finishing another thigh. Joe saw him pause and laughed.

"I ain't talkin' 'bout you. You work. And the work you're doin' now, lookin' for those worthless cowboys, that's good work."

John took a deep breath and resumed eating his chicken. "How long did that bunch work for you?"

"Not more than a couple of months." Joe paused as he gathered his thoughts. "I never felt good about them three. I was afraid they were no good when I met them but I believe in givin' a man a chance to prove himself. And I gave 'em about two months 'til I realized they weren't gonna change. They were long on talk, eager to fight, and hungry all the time. And they only worked half-way.

114

They were always the last to go to work and the first to quit. And any time there was a new job, you've never heard anyone complain like those three. The worst part is they were rubbin' off on the other hands. Anyone they were around seemed to get lazier and lazier so I fired all three of the worthless lot. Why are you lookin' for 'em?"

"'Cause Holloway murdered a woman in Laredo. She was a woman Slim was in love with in the past."

"You mean Marie? I can't remember the rest of her name but it was long and sounded like a song."

John swallowed more chicken and recited the name. "Her full name was Consuelo Marie De Zavala Morales. But she also took Slim's last name after she broke it off with Slim."

"So her name was Marie Hanson? I remember Slim talkin' about her on the cattle drive back in sixty-five. He was heartbroken. Slim talked about her on and off all the way to Kansas City. Why did she take Slim's name if she wasn't gonna stay with him?"

"As best as I can tell," John explained, "she was very much in love with Slim. But she knew that her Castilian parents wouldn't accept her bein' married to a gringo. She cared enough about honoring them that she was willin' to leave Slim. Shortly after that, she found out she was carryin' Slim's child and moved to Laredo so she could raise her son without bringing shame on her parents or on Slim."

"Foolish girl!" exclaimed Joseph. "Didn't she know Slim loved her and would have married her in an instant?"

"I don't know, Joe. I guess she thought she was doin' the right thing for all concerned. From what I've been able to put together, everyone who knew her liked her. She was a special woman and she has raised a remarkable son. But let's get back to Holloway. You said you fired all three of them?"

"Yup. And when I fired them no goods, I did it in front of all the hands at breakfast. I had my foreman and some other men standin' by so they wouldn't get rough. And when they left, I gave all the hands a little speech. I told 'em if they wanted to do shoddy work and complain like those three, they needed to draw their pay right then. Otherwise, I expected them to get to work and give me a full day if they expected a full day of pay."

"I'll bet that had an impact." John had become a bit self-conscious about his eating so he pushed his plate back and just listened to Joe.

"It shor did. The men got back to laughin' and havin' fun with their work. Don't get me wrong; they work hard. But they're enjoyin' their work more. The squabblin' that was goin' on stopped. I haven't heard any complaints since those three lefts."

"I tracked Holloway and his bunch to Encinal. Seems they worked there until a couple of days ago when they got fired. I was hopin' they'd come this way."

Joe shook his head. "No, they didn't come back this way. They would know better than to stop here. And I would have heard if they came this way. I've got hands out all over this country. My land is on both sides of the El Camino Real. If they came this way, they would have been seen and I'm sure the hands would have told me."

Mo interrupted the conversation. He was carrying two bowls of banana pudding. John watched as he placed the bowls before them. Both were filled to capacity. "I just got 'em out of the oven. And my feelin's will be hurt if you don't get at least one refill."

John put a big spoon of the pudding in his month and let out an audible groan. "Oh my goodness. This may be the best thing I've ever put in my mouth." John continued eating until he had scraped the bowl clean. Mo was standing back watching with satisfaction as the pudding disappeared.

As John set his spoon down, Mo scooped up his bowl, quickly refilled it and set it before John. John couldn't help but smile as he looked at the bowl of pudding, then back at Joe and then at Mo. Using a bit of restraint, he was committed to not finishing that bowlful until Joe finished his first.

Joe continued to pontificate about ranching and motivating the hands to give their best work. "… and if you give a man good grub, he has somethin' to look forward to at the end of the day."

As Joe finished his pudding, John took his last bite and pushed his bowl aside. Mo was immediately there to take the bowl back for another refill. John gave a half-hearted plea that Mo not get him any more. But when Mo brought back the third bowl, John had no trouble finishing it. This time when his bowl was empty, John held on and politely told Mo he didn't have room for any more. That was mostly true but John felt he could probably eat a bit more.

"So since they didn't come this way," Joe offered, "it must

mean they turned back toward Laredo. What are you plannin' on doin' now?

"If you'll let me bunk here tonight, at first light tomorrow, I'll head back to Laredo just as fast as my horse will carry me."

"Of course you can stay here. Just pick out a bunk. And be sure to give your horse a bucket of oats. He'll be needin' it for the trip. But in the mornin' before you leave, come by and pick up some grub. I'll tell Mo to be expectin' you."

John thanked his host and went out to the hitching rail and led Midnight over to the corral. After a good brushing, he got Midnight a bucket of oats and headed to the bunkhouse. On the way, he marveled at how a man he had only just met seemed like a lifelong friend.

That night, John slept well. He felt he had a plan in mind and was close to catching Holloway. As one of the hands blew out the lamp, John smiled to himself as he thought how much he had enjoyed his meal, especially being introduced to a new dessert.

Before first light, John was wide-awake. He slipped out of the dark bunkhouse listening to a chorus of snoring and heavy breathing. As he walked to the corral, he whistled softly once and heard Midnight reply with a whinny. After saddling his horse, he left Midnight at the hitching rail in front of the dining hall.

Inside, Mo was just finishing filling a flour sack with food. "Joe told me you were goin' after Holloway and his bunch. I hope you catch 'em."

"Thanks Mo. I feel sure I will. And thanks for the grub. It feels like you packed enough to last me a week or more." John swung up onto Midnight, hung the groceries over his saddle horn, lifted a hand to wave at Mo, and hit the trail back to El Camino Real.

Roy Clinton

Roy Clinton

CHAPTER 15

LAREDO, TEXAS

C rudder turned south when he got to El Camino Real and hoped he could make up lost time heading to Laredo. He knew Holloway never made it to Cotulla. Now instead of being only a day behind Holloway, he is at least two days behind. John dug down into the grub sack and snagged a couple of fresh biscuits. They were still warm and more tender and flavorful than any biscuits he could remember eating. He was grateful Cotulla insisted he see Mo and pick up food for the journey.

Normally Laredo was a two-day ride from Cotulla's Ranch. But John knew Midnight could make the nearly seventy miles in a day. John gave Midnight his head and the magnificent horse ran like he was on a racetrack. Every fifteen to twenty minutes, John would rein Midnight back to a walk—which the horse didn't like—and finally settle into a fast lope. After a few minutes at a reduced pace, John would once again give the gleaming black horse free rein.

John made it back to Laredo by midafternoon. He went

immediately to the sheriff's office. Sheriff Lasiter heard John riding hard to his office and came out to meet him.

"I knew it sounded like someone was riding here to tell me of an emergency. Come in John and tell me what you've found."

"Hello JD. While I'm glad to see you, I'm still after Holloway. I was just a day behind him when I got to Encinal so I figured he headed north to San Antonio. But when I got to the Cotulla Ranch, I found he had not gotten that far. He must have turned back to Laredo."

JD poured John a cup of coffee and set the mug on the desk. As John picked it up and began drinking, Lasiter filled John in on what he knew. "A couple of days ago, someone came in the office and told me they had seen Holloway, Gomez, and Atkins riding back into town. I found it hard to believe since I was sure Holloway knew I'd sworn out a warrant for his arrest. I walked down to the saloon and was told Holloway and the rest had just ridden into town on their way to Mexico."

"Thanks for the coffee, JD. I think I'll head over to the saloon and see what more I can find out." John led Midnight down the street and tied him in front of the saloon. The sign swinging from the ceiling of the porch read, Bustin' Loose Saloon and had a drawing of a cowboy riding a bronc.

As he walked into the saloon, John was aware the noise level dropped considerably. He walked to the bar and said, "Manny, could I get a beer please?"

"Sure thing, Mr. Crudder." Manny quickly poured the beer and instead of sliding it down the bar, brought it down and set it in front of John. John looked around the saloon and realized everyone was watching at him. Actually, they were gawking.

"Thanks, Manny."

"You're welcome, Mr. Crudder."

"Manny just call me John. Do you mind if I ask you something?"

"Sure Mr.—er, John."

"Why is everyone staring at me?"

"Well, sir, they heard about your fancy knife work and how quick you are on the draw. I 'spect you could say you have a reputation."

"I see. Well, I didn't want a reputation of that kind. And I certainly didn't want to kill those men."

"You didn't have any choice. I saw it all. They came after you."

"Thanks, Manny. I appreciate you makin' that clear to the sheriff. I wonder if I could ask you more about Holloway? I understood he has been back here."

"That's right. He came in with Gomez and Atkins and all three ordered whisky. They drank most of a bottle. By the way, you need to be aware, they know you're after them."

"How do they know that?"

"One of the men who was in the bar when you killed those fellers told 'em." Manny looked from side-to-side in a conspiratorial way. "He said you were a big man that was quicker on the draw than anyone he'd ever scene. He also said you had all kinds of knives coming out of your back and your sleeves and even your boots. He said you threw five knives in all. I don't think that was right but you know how people are. They tend to exaggerate a mite."

"I guess so." John nodded his head in agreement. "Any idea where they're headed?"

"When they left, they said real loud so everyone could hear that they were headed to Mexico and were going all the way to Mexico City and were gonna stay there." Once again, Manny looked side to side. "But I don't think that's where they're going."

"Why not?"

"'Cause I heard Gomez and Atkins whisperin' about goin' to San Anton. I think they just said Mexico in case you came back lookin' for 'em. That would throw you off their scent."

John laid a silver dollar on the bar beside his untouched beer. "Thanks, Manny. And if they were to come back here, I would appreciate you not mentioning I was lookin' for 'em."

Manny expertly slid the coin off the bar and into his pocket. "You can count on me, John. As far as they're concerned, you were never here."

John left the Bustin' Loose and led Midnight back to the sheriff's office. He told the sheriff of his conversation with Manny.

"So Manny don't think they headed to Mexico atall?" asked Lasiter.

"That's right. He thinks they are headed to San Anton. I guess I'll head that way and see if I can find them."

"I wish I could ride with you, John. Just remember, when you find 'em, I'm expectin' you to bring 'em back here for trial."

"I won't forget, sheriff. I intend to bring them in alive if they'll let me."

Roy Clinton

CHAPTER 16

EL CAMINO REAL

J ohn mounted Midnight and took the road out of town to the north. As he rode, he wondered how far he was behind Holloway and his gang. John rode on until he found the small lake where he camped before. He unsaddled Midnight, gave him a good grooming, and left him free to drink his fill and graze through the evening.

It didn't take John long to get a fire built and a pot of coffee started. He pulled the grub sack from his saddle horn knowing it contained a slab of bacon, thinking that would be his supper. But as he went through the bag, he found Mo had packed up around ten pieces of fried chicken. They were all thighs and legs. John smiled to himself as he realized Mo must have watched him carefully to know which pieces of chicken John favored. There was also a Mason jar of leftover mashed potatoes and gravy and several more biscuits.

John thought about trying to heat up his leftovers but after devouring two pieces of chicken, he realized he liked it just as well cold. Surprisingly, the mashed potatoes and gravy were also good cold. He made quick work of the food. In the bottom of the sack he found one more Mason jar and wondered what Mo had given him. He had to hold the container near the fire to identify its contents. John smiled as he realized Mo had sent him some more banana pudding, or as Mo called it, 'nana puddin'.

As the fire burned down, John drank another cup of coffee and wondered what tomorrow would bring. Would he find Holloway and the others? Or would he have to continue his quest on toward San Antonio? Without warning, John recalled the nightmare he had a few days earlier when a masked man had shot him several times and also shot Midnight. An involuntary shudder shook John. He pulled the collar of his coat up to give him a bit more warmth. As he rolled out his ground cloth and got his blanket, John wondered if the dream was a premonition of some coming catastrophe. He tossed and turned for a while waiting for sleep to come. When it did come, it was restless. He knew he was dreaming but he couldn't recall any of his dreams. All he knew is his sleep was troubled.

When John woke up, the sun was already high in the sky. He realized he must have finally fallen to sleep and slept soundly just before sunup. John drank his leftover coffee without heating it. He hurriedly saddled Midnight and put away his bedroll. As he swung up, he reached in the grub bag and grabbed the two remaining biscuits.

Once he finished the biscuits, John let Midnight run. He felt bad that he had slept late. He thought his horse was going to have to make up for the time he lost. Midnight ran on with abandon longer than John typically allowed.

By late afternoon, John made it into Encinal and headed over to the livery stable. The stableman recognized John and took the reins as John swung down.

"Howdy, young feller. Can I get your horse some oats? He sure seemed to like 'em when you was here before."

"Sure, that would be great." John unsaddled Midnight, got his brush and started to groom his mount.

"I can do that for you, mister."

John smiled at the old man. "Thank you kindly. But I enjoy doin' that myself."

"Suit yourself. Glad to see a man take care of his horse."

"Maybe you can help me. I'm looking for three men. One of them is missin' part of his ear and has a spider tattoo on his hand. And one of the men has a fancy hat with a hatband made of silver pesos."

"Yup, I've seen em," said the stableman. "The other man is a Meskin. Yeah, they've been here. They are up to no good, I can tell you that."

John stopped brushing and looked at the old man. "What do you mean?"

"Anyone who would treat their horses the way they do, are up to no good. That I know."

"What did they do?" John asked.

"They'd ridden their horses too hard and were too lazy to do anything to take care of them. I don't think they had given 'em any water all day. They just left 'em here and walked over to the saloon."

John listened carefully to the old man. "When were they here?"

"Yesterday. Came through here 'bout this same time. I offered to get their horses some oats, but they said they didn't deserve anything more than hay. What kind of person will treat a horse like that?"

John finished brushing Midnight and flipped the old man a silver dollar. "Would you please give my horse some oats? And if you don't mind, I'll bunk down beside him in his stall."

The stableman smiled as he pocketed the coin. "Shor 'nough, mister. Glad to take care of your horse. Help yourself to sleeping with your horse." He moved back toward John and added in a bit of a whisper. "For another half a dollar, I can get you a cot to sleep on."

"Thanks, but I'll be fine on the hay." The old man's face reflected his sadness at John's response. "Come to think about it, I'll take you up on that cot." John reached in his pocket and found a fifty-cent piece and flipped it high in the air. The old man smiled as he quickly caught it and put it in his pocket.

Crudder walked over to the saloon and took a seat at the same table he had eaten at a few days before. No sooner had he taken a seat than Ruby walked out of the kitchen with two plates of food and brought them over to John's table.

"Steak and taters sound all right to you, John?"

"How did you get that ready so fast?"

"I was standin' out front of the saloon when I saw you ride into town. I figured you'd be headed this way. Mind if I join you? I was just getting' ready to have my supper."

"That would be fine, Miss Ruby."

"Now don't start that 'Miss Ruby' nonsense, cowboy. I'll go get our beer and be right back."

In less than a minute she was back with two mugs and started digging into her steak. "Better eat up, John. You're gonna need your strength. Yes, you sure will."

"The food's good, Ruby. What do you mean, I'm gonna need my strength?"

Ruby fowled the air with a number of colorful words she used to describe Holloway and his men. "Cause I know why you're here. Holloway and his gang are in town. That is, they were in town yesterday. I think they headed out to the Dawson Ranch."

"Why would that do that? They were fired just before I came through here earlier."

"Well that's why they're going out there. They think Colby owes them more than he paid them when he fired 'em. And that's not all. They know all about you. They know you're huntin' 'em down for murdering Marie Hanson. John, you better be careful. I think those boys are as dangerous as they come. It wouldn't bother them one bit to kill you and cut you up into tiny little pieces."

John considered Ruby's words as he continued to eat. They talked throughout the meal but the only thing on John's mind was that he was close to catching Holloway. When he finished eating, John paid for their meals and left Ruby a nice tip.

He walked over to the livery and found the old man had set up a cot with a mattress in the stall next to Midnight. There was also a pillow and two blankets. John smiled to himself as he realized he was going to enjoy having a good bed under him that evening.

When John got out to the Dawson Ranch the next morning, he couldn't find anyone. There were horses saddled but no sign of the hands. John swung down and looped the reins around the hitching rail in front of the bunkhouse. No one was in the bunkhouse, so John walked through it and out the back door. Just down from the bunkhouse, John saw a gathering of hands beneath a large oak tree.

John walked over to where the men were gathered. He removed his hat as he realized he was witnessing a funeral. Actually, he saw three graves.

"Ashes to ashes and dust to dust. The Lord hath given and the Lord hath taken away. Blessed be the name of the Lord." As the parson spoke those words he tossed a handful of dirt onto the coffins. There was a mumbling among the cowboys and they put on their hats and started walking away from the grave.

John overheard one cowboy. "The Lord may have given but he didn't take away. That was Holloway's doin'." John walked up beside them to get the story.

"You mean this is Holloway's work?" asked John.

"Yup. He rode in with his gang yesterday mornin'. They went into the ranch house and killed Dawson and his wife. They shot Dawson's daughter. It looks like she'll live. Then they came out to the bunkhouse and shot Colby. One of the men was just coming in and saw all three of them standing over Colby's bed. Colby was still laid up with the busted leg from that snake trick they played on him. He didn't even have a gun. They just kept shootin' him. As they mounted up and rode off, Holloway shouted back, "That's what Colby gets for firin' us. And anybody who comes after us will get the same thing."

John was stunned by level of violence brought on by Holloway and his fellow outlaws. "Any idea where they headed?" asked John.

"Nah," responded the same hand. "They took the road back to town but there's no tellin' where they went from there."

John saddled up and rode back to Encinal. He rode up to the saloon, swung down, and wrapped the reins over the hitching rail. John walked over to Ruby who was startled to see him.

"Since you're here, I take it you found Holloway."

"Yes, I found where they've been. Did they come back here?" asked John.

"They were here early this morning. I'm surprised you didn't run into them on your way to the Dawson Ranch."

"I left pretty early. They must have been camped off the road. They killed Dawson and his wife and shot their daughter."

Ruby gasped at the news. She let fly with a string of profanity about Holloway and his bunch. "Why would they hurt that little girl? Did they kill her?"

"I didn't see her but I was told they think she'll live. They also killed Colby."

Ruby bowed her head as her anger gave way to grief. Tears flowed from her eyes. "Colby was as good as they come. They didn't have no reason to hurt him. He was one of the best men I know."

John listened as Ruby continued talking about her friendship with Colby. Shortly the tears stopped and she was once again flinging profanities into the air about Holloway, Gomez, and Atkins. "There haven't been three more worthless men that ever lived. John I hope you catch 'em. And when you do, I hope you will kill 'em all."

"Ruby, you can rest assured I'll do all I can to catch 'em. But when I do, I'm planning on bringin' in so they can stand trial. They've got a lot to answer for."

"I know you're right in that, John. Don't let me keep you. Go find those...." Once again Ruby cut loose with words that questioned the outlaw's parentage, masculinity, and value as human beings. John marveled at the wide variety of Ruby's colorful vocabulary.

John walked out of the saloon and down to the sheriff's office, leaving Midnight at the saloon. He walked into the office and introduced himself to Sheriff Grayson.

"So what can I do for you, Mr. Crudder?"

"Sheriff Grayson, I just came from the Dawson Ranch. Jasper Holloway, and two of his accomplices just murdered Dawson and his wife, shot their daughter and murdered Colby, their foreman."

"What? That can't be. I saw Dawson yesterday mornin' and he was fine."

"Be that as it may, Sheriff. He and his wife are dead now. And so is Colby. I just came from their funerals." John told the account he had heard at the ranch and how all three men had stood over Colby and shot him multiple times because he fired them.

"Sheriff, you need to know I'm after Holloway for another killin'. He murdered the mother of a friend of mine down in Laredo. I plan to take 'em to Laredo to stand trial."

"You can't do that Mr. Crudder. You have to bring 'em here. They need to stand trial here for their crimes in this county. This is where they belong."

"I can understand how you feel. Sheriff JD Lasiter in Laredo wanted to deputize me as I hunted for Holloway but I declined. I used to be the marshal in Bandera. I know I can bring these men in but I don't want anyone tellin' me how to do it and where to take 'em. So sheriff, they're goin' to be taken to Laredo. I'll be sure to tell Sheriff Lasiter that when Laredo is through with 'em, if they're still alive, you want to have a crack at all three here in Encinal."

"I guess that'll have to do, Mr. Crudder. I'll ride out to the ranch and get statements from the hands and from anyone who knows anything about the murders. Do you know which way Holloway went?"

"I'm not sure but I'm headed toward San Anton. My hunch is they are headed back there."

"Well I hope you find 'em," said the sheriff.

"Oh, I'll find 'em all right. I just hope they let me take them back to Laredo. If they don't, I'll bury 'em alone the way."

Roy Clinton

CHAPTER 17

Midnight took John out of Encinal and headed north. Crudder allowed his horse to move into a full gallop as he cleared town. He had traveled just a few miles when he saw someone had tied some horses in the shade of a tree not far off the road. John pulled Midnight up quickly, not wanting to reveal his presence before he was sure what he was dealing with.

He took Midnight well off the road and swung down. Midnight didn't make a sound. It was as if the mighty horse picked up on John's stealth and followed suit. He left Midnight tied to a tree, pulled his six-gun and headed toward the place where the other horses were tied.

As John got closer, he stopped and watched from behind a tree. He saw the three horses were saddled and ready to ride but he didn't see any people. John waited, hoping the owners of the horses would soon come into view. He hunched down so he would be partially hidden by the tall grass.

As he waited he thought he saw movement to his right. As he turned toward it, he thought he also saw movement to his left. John dropped lower into the grass and held perfectly still. Then John heard something behind him. It was then he realized he had ridden into a trap. The sound behind him seemed closer and a greater threat so he turned to face what he was sure would be a gunman. As he did, gunshots came from every direction.

He felt the impact of the bullets. One tore into his right leg and another into his right arm. "I got him," said a voice. "So did I," said another voice.

John passed his gun to his left hand. While not being truly ambidextrous, he knew he was a good marksman with his left hand. As he raised the gun to take a bead on one of the men who shot him, he felt a bullet strike him in the head. His last thought was I never even heard it coming!

"I got him," said Holloway. "Shot him right in the head."

"I got him too!" said Gomez. Got him in his right arm. He couldn't shoot with the bullet in his arm.

"I shot him in the leg," said Atkins. "Knock the legs out from under your prey. That way they can't get away.

"You guys keep congratulating yourselves," said Holloway. "I got him in the head. If you want to kill someone, that's the way you do it. Now let's get out of here before someone rides along the road."

"What do we do with his body?" asked Atkins. "Want to bury him?"

Holloway let out a bitter laugh. "I'm not strainin' my back on digging a grave for this man. If you two want to bury him, be my guests. I'm headed on north. We need to get out of this country. Let the buzzards clean up our mess."

The men laughed at Holloway's coldness. They mounted up and took the trail north toward the Cotulla Ranch. Crudder lay right where he fell. It didn't take the buzzards long to start circling. Their sharp eyes and sense of smell immediately focused on their next meal.

Roy Clinton

CHAPTER 18

ENCINAL, TEXAS

S heriff Grayson rode out to the Dawson Ranch and took statements from everyone who knew anything about the murders. He found it hard to believe anyone could be as coldblooded as Holloway and his henchmen.

Leaving the ranch, he rode back to the El Camino Real and turned north to see if he could pick up the trail of the murderers. He traveled a few miles out of town and realized he was not able to distinguish between the many horse tracks on the road. The sheriff was just getting ready to turn around when he saw Midnight standing sentinel over Crudder's body.

Sheriff Grayson rode over to John and swung down. He saw John was covered in blood and had obviously been shot several times. The sheriff was sad as he thought about the eagerness of the young man in his office that morning and how he had been cut down by the very outlaws he was chasing.

Just then, he heard John let out a moan. The sheriff got his canteen from his saddle horn and put the water to John's lips.

"Ooooh! My head!" John tried to move but the sheriff pressured him to the ground.

"John, I can't believe you're alive. Better lay still. You've been shot several times and the hole is your head is bleedin' badly. Let me get your hat off so I can see how bad it is."

Sheriff Grayson careful removed John's hat and inspected the wound. It looked to him like it was a glancing blow. Grayson picked up John's hat and looked at it. As he inspected it he found something stuck in the headliner. There were two tintypes stacked on top of each other. One showed a young woman and the other was of two little girls.

"Well, John, it looks like your family has saved your life." He showed the badly damaged tintypes to Crudder. John tried to smile but the pain in his head was too great.

"I remember putting them there just this mornin'. They were in my pocket but I thought I might take better care of them puttin' 'em in my hat. Turns out, that just destroyed both of them."

"And saved your life," said the sheriff. "That and your hard head. Now hold still. I've got to get the bleeding stopped in your scalp wound or you will be dead soon."

The sheriff skillfully tied his bandana around John's head, stanching the bleeding. He then went to his saddlebag and dug out another bandana and tied it to John's injured shoulder. He then reached up and untied the bandana around John's neck and tied it around John's leg.

"John, do you think you can ride if I help you into the saddle?"

"I think I can. Bring Midnight over here and I'll be able to get in the saddle by myself." The sheriff brought Crudder's horse nearby and John tried to stand but collapsed to the ground.

"This time let me help you, mister hardhead!" The sheriff held John's left arm and got him over to Midnight. John reached up and took hold of the saddle horn as the sheriff boosted him up. With great effort, John swung his injured leg over the saddle and sat up. The pain was so great that he couldn't remain sitting up straight but bent over the saddle horn.

"Let me see the reins, John. I'll lead your horse back into town. We're not going fast. You let me know if we need to stop."

"I'll be fine, Sheriff."

Sheriff Grayson mounted up and led Midnight back into Encinal, stopping in front of the saloon. He helped John off his horse and supported him as he walked him through the swinging doors.

"What! What happened to him?" Ruby immediately ran to John's side. "I'll bet those sidewinders did this to him. John, did that no-account Holloway do this?"

John tried to reply but he was too weak.

"Ruby, do you have room upstairs for Crudder?"

"Of course, Sheriff. Bring him on up. The room next to mine is empty. Let's get him up there and I'll nurse him back to health." They half carried John up the stairs and got him into bed. With great care, Ruby pulled John's boots off and then started inspecting his wounds.

"The shots to his arm and leg went clean through. Let me get some whisky out of my room. I need to clean 'em up." Ruby hurried next door and came back with a half-empty bottle. John let out a howl each time she poured the alcohol into his wounds. "Roll him over sheriff. I've got to pour some whisky in the other side. Sugar, I know this hurts, and you cry out if you need to, but you know I've got to do this for your own good."

She continued tending the wounds and John managed to contain his outcries and only groan. Once those wounds were dressed, she turned to the wound on his head. "Sugar, this one's gonna need stitching' up. You've got a long gash that won't quit bleedin' if I don't stitch it up. Good thing you've got a hard head or you'd be dead now."

"It weren't just his hard head." The sheriff pulled the ruined tintypes from his pocket. "He had these in his headband. I think they probably saved his life."

Ruby inspected the photos. "Sugar, you've got a fine lookin' family. And the good thing is, you're gonna get to see 'em again. Sheriff, I need you to stay here with our patient while I go get a needle and thread. Now, Sugar, don't you go nowhere while I'm gone." Ruby let out a loud laugh at her little joke.

She was back in a couple of minutes with her seamstress supplies, some bandages and a small bottle of ointment. Taking a seat on the side of his bed, she held up her bottle of whisky. "Sugar, you might want to take a couple of pulls on the bottle before I get started. It's gonna hurt right smart."

John shook his head. "No, I'll be fine. I've had stitches before."

"Sugar, I hope you're right. This is gonna hurt like…." John smiled to himself as he heard yet another colorful description from Ruby. He realized he heard many more swear words from her than he had from any man.

Ruby carefully washed her hands in the washbasin. John was impressed she used soap. She then poured some whisky in a bowl and completely submerged the needle with the thread attached. "All right, Sugar. Here we go."

Ruby used scissors to cut John's hair that was near the gash. She then made quick work of the stitches, taking care to not let any loose hair remain in the wound. When she finished, she used one corner of a cotton handkerchief she had up her sleeve to apply more whisky and then used the rest of the cloth to apply the ointment. She then wrapped the bandage around John's head to finish her job.

"There you go, Sugar. You'll be good as new in a few days. I want you to try to sleep now. I'll bring you some supper later, but I want you to rest until then.

✳ ✳ ✳

John did his best to be a good patient. He stayed in bed for the better part of a week. Toward the end of the week, he was strong enough to come down stairs for his meals. Ruby turned out to be a first-rate nurse. During that time, it was obvious to John, she had taken to treating him as she would her own son. While he didn't like convalescing, John made the best of it and decided it did make more sense to try to heal up before he started out after Holloway.

After ten days, John just couldn't stand being idle. He announced to Ruby he would be leaving in the morning. She did her best to talk him out of it, saying he needed at least two more weeks to heal up. While he knew she was right, he also knew he needed to get on the trail of Holloway and his gang before he lost complete track of them.

When morning came, John went downstairs to find Ruby had cooked him some fried eggs, sausage, and biscuits. He hungrily ate everything she put on his plate and used his last biscuit to mop up anything that remained.

Ruby sat down with him as he was finishing his meal. "I want you to know you're goin' against Nurse Ruby's orders. I don't think you should travel."

"I know you don't, Ruby. But I've got to get after Holloway before the trail gets cold."

"I guess so." She picked up a small sack and handed it to John. "I made you a little something to eat on the trail."

"Thanks, Ruby. What did you make?"

She winked at John and said, "Well, Sugar, you know we only serve steak and taters."

John smiled and accepted a hug from the woman who was determined to see him return to full health. "You catch those critters and bring 'em back here on your way to Laredo. I need to have a few words with them."

He tipped his hat and went to the livery stable where Midnight was already saddled and ready to go. He made a mental note not to stop at Encinal when he traveled back with the outlaws. While he would love to see the people in the town, he wasn't sure he could keep his prisoners safe. And he was sure Sheriff Grayson would lay claim to them and not allow him to move them on to Laredo.

CHAPTER 19

EL CAMINO REAL

T he bullet wounds surprisingly didn't give John as much pain as he was expecting. His head was another matter. Ruby had offered to send some laudanum with him but John declined. She gave him some willow bark and told him to chew it saying it would help with the headaches. John found it did help but he still had a dull headache most of the time.

He headed to Cotulla hoping to make it by nightfall. His headaches were so great that he realized he needed to break from traveling. John camped for the night and on his second day out of Encinal made it to Cotulla. Arriving at the ranch just after noon, John found Joe and Mo deep in conversation.

John swung down and went into the dining hall. "What on earth has happened to you?" asked Joe. "Looks like you got shot up." John carefully took off his hat and hobbled over to a chair and sat down.

"I found Holloway and his gang. They shot me and left me for dead."

"It looks like they came close to killin' you," said Mo, as he scampered back to the kitchen to get John something to eat.

"John, they been through here," said Joseph. "It was nearly two weeks ago they rode past here. They didn't come on to the ranch. They knew I wouldn't take kindly to 'em bein' here. One of the hands spotted them. He doesn't think they saw him. They were headed north."

Mo arrived with a bowl of beef stew and several pieces of cornbread. "Thanks Mo," said John as he took a bite of the stew. "This is wonderful. I hate to hurry on but I need to eat and get out of here. I've got to catch up to Holloway."

"That don't make sense, John," said Joe. "They're two weeks ahead of you. Stay the night and rest a spell. You can leave out in the morning."

John continued to shovel the stew into his mouth and mop his bowl with the cornbread. "I 'preciate that, Joe. I know that would be the smart thing to do. But I just can't take any more time out. I've already been layin' up for the past two weeks. I've got to get back on the trail."

Joe nodded in agreement. "I know you do. Just take care of yourself, John. You're not gonna do any good at all if you catch them again and can't survive the encounter."

John shook hands with his two friends and gently placed his hat on his wounded head as he walked out of the dining hall. Swinging up onto Midnight was still very painful. Slowly, he made his way into the saddle. He touched the brim of his hat as he saluted the two men and turned north toward Darlington.

The ride to Darlington was uneventful except for the tremendous pain John felt each time Midnight's hoofs touched the ground. His head pounded with each step. His arm and leg throbbed but so far he hadn't reopened any of the wounds.

As nightfall approached, he could see the general store ahead. That store was the only business in town. There were only two houses on the only road through town. John supposed there were other farms and ranches around that supported the need for the store.

John went on past the store and to a grove of trees just off the road. It was just beginning to rain so John knew he was in for a wet night. He unsaddled Midnight and gave him a good brushing and then gathered enough branches to make a small fire. Fortunately the wood he gathered was still dry enough that he was able to light it easily. He was just getting his coffee makings ready when he heard a voice behind him.

"Howdy," shouted a man. John jumped. He was startled he had not heard the approaching man. He couldn't see the man's face, but he was wearing a long yellow slicker coat that went down past the tops of the man's boots.

"Howdy back to 'ya."

"Stranger, you're gonna get mighty wet before the night's over."

By then, the rain had started in earnest. John watched as his fledgling fire flickered and went out. He realized with all his travels, this was the first time he had to contend with more than just a light, short-lived shower.

"Grab your saddle and horse and follow me to the barn behind my house." The stranger turned and walked away. John wasted no time in following the man down the road a few yards and around to his barn. The stranger in the yellow slicker lit a lamp and pointed to the back corner of the barn. By the time he got to the barn, John was soaked to the bone. Still he was grateful for having a dry place to spend the night.

"You can put your horse in the stall back there. There's plenty of hay. Sorry but I don't have any oats."

"A little hay will be fine," John replied. "Thanks mister. I certainly 'preciate your hospitality. That would have been a miserable night out in the rain."

"Get your horse settled and come on in the house. My wife has supper ready. She told me to bring you in for a hot meal. It's just beans and cornbread but its good food."

Without waiting for an answer, the man turned and walked back into the rain. John put Midnight into the stall, gave him some hay and water and turned out the lamp. He pulled his collar up and ran for the house. As his boots connected with the porch, the front door of the house opened.

"Come in this house. You're going to catch your death out there." The little lady held a lamp high in one hand and held the door with the other. John checked his boots for mud and then wiped them on the mat at the door. As he entered the house he took his hat from his head.

"My goodness, child! What happened to you?" As she looked at the bandage on John's head, she came close and her fingers traced the outline of the blood-tinged pad that covered his wound.

"I'm sorry, ma'am, I'm so unpresentable. I can only guess how I look. Actually, that's just a little place that has a few stitches in it." John winced as he tried to raise his right arm to his head.

"Hubert, get his shirt off of him. He's hurt. And I saw him limping. What's happened to you, son?"

"I don't mean to be any trouble ma'am. I got shot a few times but I'm much better now. It's been more than two weeks since it happened so I'm mostly healed up."

"Poppycock! You're definitely not healed up. Hubert, get his shirt off so I can see his arm."

"All right Etta Mae. I'm doin' it."

As John pulled his shirt off, he saw the shock on their faces as they looked at the scabbard with the dagger on his right forearm. When his shirt was completely off, Etta Mae sucked in a loud breath and quickly clamped a hand over her mouth. John realized she was looking at the double scabbard on his back that held matching daggers.

"Are you an outlaw, son?"

"No ma'am. In fact, I used to be a lawman. I got used to wearing these when I was the marshal in Bandera. I guess I've never felt fully dressed without them ever sense."

Etta Mae looked at John as though she was trying to see into his soul. After a full minute of staring at John, she said, "Hubert, there's no use staring at the boy. I think he's a good man. If he feels better having those knives on him, that's none of our business. What's your name, son?"

"My name is John, ma'am. I didn't mean for my knives to startle you. And really, I'm doin' much better. There's no need to bother. Like I said, I think I'm about healed up."

Crudder waited awkwardly as Etta Mae took the old bandages off his head and his arm. "These are infected! When is the last time you changed the bandages?"

"I don't reckon I've changed 'em since I left Encinal two or three days ago."

"These need to be changed every day if you don't want to get blood poisoning."

"Yes ma'am. I recall bein' told that. I just hadn't thought of it since then."

"Hubert, go get him some dry clothes. He can't wear these wet things."

"That's all right, ma'am. I have some dry clothes in my saddlebags."

"You heard him, Hubert. Go get his saddlebags and bring them in here."

Hubert put his slicker back on and headed out to the barn. He was back in a few minutes with the saddlebags. Etta Mae continued cleaning the arm and leg wounds and applying new bandages.

"John, you need to get your pants off now," said Etta Mae.

"Ma'am, my leg is fine, really."

"I'm sure it's doing just as well your scalp and arm."

John realized he was on the losing end of the argument so he didn't reply.

"I can see you're modest, so I'll turn my back until you get your pants off and can get yourself covered. Hubert, pull the boy's boots off. He can't do it himself with all those bullet holes in him."

Hubert knew better than to argue so he did as instructed. John slipped out of his trousers and gratefully accepted the blanket Hubert offered. He barely covered himself when Etta Mae turned back around and started working on his thigh wound.

"You're lucky. Your leg is healing fine. Let me get you bandaged up and then you can put your pants back on." Etta Mae gently tended the wound and wrapped a fresh bandage around it. She backed up and admired her work. "There, you're all fixed up. I'm going back to finishing up supper while you get dressed. Hubert, you set the table and then get a pallet out for John. I'm not having him going back to that old barn tonight and mess up my doctoring. John, you'll sleep in here by the fire. I hope that works all right for you. We don't have another bed."

"That'll be just fine, ma'am. I shor 'preciate all you're doin' for me. I didn't mean to be so much trouble."

"You hush now. It's just the right thing to do."

Etta Mae took off her apron and set a big cast iron pot of beans on the table. Next she pulled the pan of cornbread from the oven and placed a plate of butter beside it. "Take a seat right there." John did as he was told and watched her as she took a cloth and placed it in her lap. Hubert did the same so John followed suit. "Hubert say grace, please."

Hubert bowed his head and did as his wife instructed. "Lord, we thank thee for the food and for our guest. A-men."

Etta Mae filled a bowl with beans and passed it to John. She then filled Hubert's and her bowls. "John would you like a piece of cornbread?"

"Yes ma'am, please." She used a spatula to serve John and her husband and then passed the plate of butter. John buttered his cornbread and took a bite of it to chase the beans he had just put in his mouth.

"Ma'am, this is wonderful. I've never tasted beans so good. And the cornbread is delicious."

Etta Mae beamed with delight. Not wanting to be outdone, Hubert added. "You shor haven't lost your touch, Etta Mae. You're the best cook in Darlington."

"You old fool. You know there's less than ten women around these parts. That's not much of a compliment."

Hubert was opening his mouth to try to repair any damage he had done, when he saw Etta Mae wink at him. It was obvious to John she was engaging in a bit of good-natured ribbing.

John laughed in spite of his effort not to. Etta Mae and Hubert joined and they all laughed with gusto.

"John, we needed a good laugh. Thanks for helping us to lighten things up a bit. I didn't catch your last name."

"It's Crudder, ma'am. John Crudder."

"Pleased to meet you Mr. Crudder. I'm Etta Mae and this is

Hubert Holloway."

John was shocked as the heard the name Holloway.

"What's wrong, son?" asked Etta Mae. "You look like you've just seen a ghost."

"I'm sorry, ma'am. I'm sure it's just a coincidence but the man who shot me was named Holloway."

Etta Mae put her hand to her mouth and said, "Hubert. Do you think that was your brother?"

"What's the man's full name," asked Hubert.

"Jasper Holloway but people call him Percy."

"Oh, Hubert! This is terrible. I'm so sorry John. Percy has always been the black sheep of the family."

Hubert got up from the table and walked to the door and hung his head. John was stunned by what he and heard. How could a couple that was so good and generous be related to such a lowlife as Jasper Holloway?

John stared at his plate as he wondered what he should say or do. Hubert came back to the table, took a seat and turned to John.

"My brother is no good. He was just by here just over a week ago. He wanted supplies from the store. I told him he was not welcome and I wouldn't sell him anything. He just laughed at me and then he and the two men with him got off their horses and proceeded to take what they wanted from the store. They just rode off without even offerin' to pay. It doesn't surprise me that he was the one that shot you. I'm just sorry he hurt you. Why do you suppose he shot you?"

"He did it because he knows I'm tracking him for murdering a woman in Laredo."

Etta Mae once again covered her mouth with both of her hands. She let out a little cry and shook her head in disbelief. She turned to John and asked, "Who is the woman he killed?"

"She was the mother of my wife's brother. He was lookin' to rob her and shot her in front of her fifteen-year-old son."

Hubert spoke up. "John, it don't surprise me none. Percy never did think like other people. What I know about him is that he don't have no conscious. Never did. If he wants somethin', he takes it. And if someone takes exception to that, he'll hurt them—or worse. That's why I didn't do anything when he and his men stole from my store. I knew he wouldn't hesitate to kill me or even Etta Mae. John, I hope you catch him and that he pays for his crimes."

"I'm gonna do my best, Hubert. I never figured on someone like him havin' family, especially a family as kind as you. I hate that I'm goin' after your kinfolk. Somehow it doesn't seem right to me."

"John, what you're doing is the right thing. Who are the men that are ridin' with Percy?

"The one with the fancy hatband is Gomez. The man with the limp is Adkins. I don't know much about them except that they have been ridin' with Percy for a while. They are all wanted for bank robbery. They killed several guards. No tellin' what else they've done."

Hubert continued questioning John. "What are you plannin' on doin' when you catch 'em?"

John stopped and considered his answer. "I have always been

convinced the right thing to do is to take them down to Laredo to stand trial. I'm still plannin' on doin' that. But I'm not gonna let my guard down and get surprised by them again. What I know is I'll defend myself and I'll not hesitate to do so. I'm only sorry Percy is your brother."

"Don't be, John. Until Percy is in prison or dead, he is gonna keep hurtin' and killin' and robbin' folks. He's a bad one. You do whatever you need to do to stop him.

"All right," said Etta Mae. "That's enough conversation about these unsavory things. It's time to eat. John finish up that bowl so I can get you some more. You know it will hurt my feelings if you don't have at least two more bowlfuls."

John laughed. "I'll do my best not to hurt your feelings. May I have some more cornbread?"

Hubert smiled for he knew his wife got great joy in having other people enjoy her cooking. He dug into his bowl of beans, delighted not to have to focus on his brother. Etta Mae refilled the bowls of both men and replenished their cornbread. John did as instructed and ate three bowlfuls.

"I hope you men have some room left. I have a peach cobbler in the oven. Now don't get excited. You know this is not peach season. It's made with canned peaches but I think it will still be good."

John licked his lips in anticipation and finished up the last of his beans and cornbread.

"I'll get you some clean bowls for the cobbler."

"Honey, I don't need one. And look at John's bowl. It looks like it just came out of the cupboard."

All three laughed at Hubert's comment. John looked at his bowl and knew it was true. He had used his cornbread to clean up every bit of bean residue.

The peach cobbler was wonderful. John reflected on how different the night had turned out from how it started. After dinner, Hubert went out on the porch and rolled a smoke. John helped clean the table and insisted on washing dishes. Etta Mae relented and allowed their new friend to help out.

"This has been hard on Hubert."

"Ma'am?"

"This talk about his brother. Hubert has always been ashamed of him and has tried to be a good influence on Percy. The truth is Percy doesn't want to change. It took Hubert a long time to accept that. But he's finally realized there is nothing he can do to make Percy change the way he lives. I hope you catch him. The sooner he pays for his crimes, the sooner Hubert can go on with his life."

John listened as he washed the dishes. He added some more hot water to the pan and tried to concentrate on the task at hand. There was nothing he could say that seemed appropriate. He just nodded his head as Etta Mae told of the sadness Hubert's brother had brought on the family.

When it was bedtime, Etta Mae put down a pallet near the fire and insisted that John allow her to pull off his boots. John was grateful for the warmth of the fire and of having dry clothes. Etta May hung up his wet clothes so they would dry by morning.

* * *

John was still sleeping when he became aware of the smell of bacon frying. He got up and rolled his pallet.

"Wake up sleepy head," said Etta Mae. "Hubert went out to check on your horse. He knew you would want to get an early start. The rain has stopped and it looks like it will be a good day. Breakfast will be ready in a few minutes. Feel free to use the washstand on the back porch. And you'll see the outhouse out back."

John pulled his boots on and followed Etta Mae's directions. When he got outside he saw Hubert. "Mornin', Hubert."

"Mornin', John. I got your horse saddled. I know it can't be easy to do with that bullet hole in your arm."

"Thanks. You're shor right. I never knew how difficult things could be with my messed-up arm. When we finish breakfast, would you mind opening your store so I could get a few things?"

"I can do that now. Etta Mae won't have breakfast done for a few minutes. What are you lookin' for?"

"Well, I'd like to buy a slicker like yours if you have one. I also need a couple of blankets and a few cans of beans."

"I've got all that. Come on in and let's get you fixed up."

John followed Hubert into the store and began browsing through the dry goods while Hubert filled his order. "I like this sideboard. I can't say I've ever seen one like it."

"I just got that in from North Carolina. It's actually a grocer's counter but they have been finding homes as sideboards. Etta Mae has wanted it for the house but she knows we can't afford it. Someday, she'll get one.

John continued to admire the piece of furniture. It was made of natural pine and was about seven feet long. It had rounded ends and a thick butcher-block top that was held together with a metal band. There were three rows of drawers and an open section below each drawer.

"Here's your slicker and blankets. There's no charge for the beans. Will there be anything else?"

"Just one thing more. I want to buy this sideboard for Etta Mae. But I don't want you to tell her about it until I leave."

"John, I—I don't know what to say. You can't do that. That's too much…"

"Hubert, I'll tell you what to say. Just say, 'thanks' and let me have a bit of pleasure in paying back you and your wife for your hospitality."

Hubert graciously put out his hand and said, "Thanks, John."

"You're welcome, Hubert. You're a kind man and you've got a good wife. I'm happy to have made your acquaintance."

The men returned to the house and ate the breakfast Etta Mae had prepared. When the meal was finished, John tied his slicker and blankets on his saddle behind the cantle and then added his saddlebags.

As he was getting ready to get into the saddle, Etta Mae gave him a big hug, being sure not to squeeze his injured arm. "John, any time you come by this way, you be sure to come at meal time. You're always welcome."

John hugged her back and shook Hubert's hand and Hubert boosted John into the saddle. "So long folks. Thanks for your hospitality."

"Good bye, John," said the couple as Midnight adopted a gentle lope. John was about a hundred yards down the road when he heard Etta Mae scream. Then she said, "John Crudder. What on earth did you do?" Then she let out a loud "whoop!"

John smiled to himself and marveled that such a relatively small gift could bring such happiness. He rode on wondering what he would face that day. Frio City was about sixteen miles ahead. He figured he should make it by noon.

Roy Clinton

CHAPTER 20

When John reached Frio City it was well before noon. John stopped in front of the livery stable to see if there had been any sign of Holloway.

"Howdy, young man," said the stableman. "Are you back to give your horse some of my oats. You know I've got the sweetest oats in these parts."

John laughed. "Yup, I think Midnight could use some oats. While he's eatin' I wonder if you could help me with some information?"

"Be glad to if I can. What you want to know?"

"I've been tracking three bad men. One is named Holloway. He's ridin' a flea-bit gray. Then there's a man with a fancy silver hatband that's ridin' a bay and another man who's walking with a limp and ridin' a dun. They were probably through here about two weeks ago."

"Yup, I seen 'em. But it weren't two weeks ago. They came through here no more than two days ago."

John listened and was visibly excited to hear that he was so much closer to the evil men. "When did they leave here?"

"Well, I think it was about dusk the day before yesterday. Yup, that's when it was. I remember 'cause they took exception to me chargin' 'em for the feed their horses ate. All I charged them was two bits each for feed and two bits for stabling them over night. They just laughed at me and didn't pay me nothin'. Men like that ought to be horse whipped."

"I agree with you on that. Which way did they go?"

The stableman pointed north. "Didn't say where they were goin' but they weren't in much of a hurry. I saw 'em when they rode out of town but they didn't go then. They went over to the saloon and didn't come out 'til near midnight. I don't sleep real sound like. Couldn't help but hear 'em when they left the saloon. They were drunker than Cooter Brown. They left their horses saddled all that time waitin' in front of the saloon. Why would anyone treat a horse like that? If they wasn't gonna leave when they picked the horses up, why didn't they just wait until they were ready to go?"

"So when they left the saloon, they headed north?"

"That's right. They probably didn't get far before they stopped for the night. Like I said. They were not in any shape to ride anywhere."

John gave two silver dollars to the stableman. "That'll make up for what they stole from you. I'm glad you didn't tangle with 'em. They've hurt a lot of people." John swung up onto Midnight.

"Thanks mister. But your horse hasn't finished his oats."

John turned in the saddle. "I'll be back this way and let him eat then." Midnight was already making time getting out of town.

Once he passed the last building, John gave Midnight his head and the big horse headed toward Moore, Texas.

He arrived in the early afternoon and swung down in front of the saloon. John tied midnight to the hitching rail and went inside and ordered a beer.

As the bartender slid the beer down to John, John asked about Holloway and his gang

"Why are you wantin' to know?" asked the barman. "You a friend of theirs?"

The corner of John's mouth turned up in a sardonic smile. "They're no friends of mine. Fact is, they shot me and left me for dead. They're also all wanted for bank robbery and murder. So have you seen them or not?"

"Sorry mister. I didn't mean nothin' by that. I just wanted to make sure you weren't with them, that's all. Yeah, they were here. They picked a fight with one old cowboy. I think they would have killed him if I hadn't got my shotgun on 'em. I told 'em to clear out and they left."

"When was that?" asked John.

"That was just last night."

John put a quarter on the bar and ran out to Midnight."

"Hey mister. Aren't you gonna drink your beer?"

John ducked under the hitching rail and pulled himself into the saddle. He pointed Midnight north, leaned forward in the saddle and moved the reins several inches in front of the saddle horn. Midnight immediately ran at full speed out of town. John was close to catching up with Holloway. He knew it would likely only be a little while until he confronted them.

John let Midnight run at full speed hoping to catch up with Holloway and his men before they hurt more people. In well less than an hour, John got to Nicksville. He slowed Midnight to a trot and headed for Nicks General Store. There were three horses tied to the hitching rail. Blue was barking at the closed door. John dismounted and tied Midnight to the hitching rail.

Blue continued his panicked barking. John drew his six-gun and walked around to the back of the store. He silently opened the door and slipped inside. The three desperados had Nicks backed up to the back wall behind the counter.

"I said, we want your money," shouted Holloway. "We're gonna find it anyway. You can make it easy and tell us and, who knows, you might even live."

"Muchachos, let's cut him a leetle," said Gomez as he unsheathed a machete he wore on his belt. "I want to see him bleed."

John took several steps toward the men. "I don't think that's a good idea."

The men turned toward John. Atkins cocked his six-gun, but John shot him between the eyes before he got his gun ready to shoot. Gomez raised his machete but as he did, John withdrew the dagger from his sleeve and let it fly with deadly accuracy. It sunk into Gomez's neck just above his sternum. Both men dropped to the floor as Holloway drew his gun. Before he could shoot, Nicks picked up a cast iron skillet and brought it down heavily on Holloway's head.

John and Nicks stood for a few seconds looking at the situation and taking in what had just happened.

"I'm sure glad to see you, John Crudder. Don't know what I'd have done if you didn't come in when you did."

"These men are just pure evil," said John. "They've murdered several people. And it looks like they were getting ready to do it again."

John went to the pile of men and removed their guns and the machete. "Nicks, hold a gun on Holloway. I want to get some handcuffs on him before he wakes up. I have some in my saddlebags."

After retrieving the handcuffs, John pulled Holloway's hands behind his back and applied the cuffs to his wrists.

"Youngster, I'm glad you came equipped. What are you gonna do with this man?"

"I'm takin' him back to Laredo to stand trial for murder. But there are probably many cities that would like to put him on trial. I'm not sure what to do with his partners. Is there an undertaker around here?"

"No, but we've got a coroner who will pronounce them dead. And there's a couple of boys that live down the road that'll be tickled to dig their graves for two dollars each. And I know they have money. They took twenty-seven dollars out of my cash drawer and decided I must have some more money hidden here. That's when you came in."

"Where do we find the coroner?" asked John.

"Well that's me?" said Nicks with a big smile on his face.

"I remember you're the justice of the peace and the postmaster."

"Yup. I'm also the coroner. So let me do my coroner work. They're dead. Now help me get my twenty-seven dollars back and enough to bury 'em."

John went through the pockets of all three men and removed their money. There were several hundred dollars between them. Together Nicks and John dragged the two dead men out of the store. When they came back inside, Holloway was just regaining consciousness.

"What happened? Who hit me?"

"I did," said Nicks. "And if you're not careful, I'll hit you again."

"What have you done to my hands? Who tied me up?"

"I did." John had just retrieved his bloody dagger from the neck of Gomez. He went over to Holloway and wiped the knife on his shirt. As he did, he lingered only inches from Holloway. Leaving his dagger dangerously close to the man's neck. Holloway's eyes carefully tracked the dagger and his face showed the terror that he felt.

"Holloway, you don't deserve it but I'm gonna let you live. You'll live long enough to get to Laredo and stand trial for murdering Marie Hanson. And if you're lucky, we're gonna ride right on past Encinal. I know they'd to get their hands on you for murdering Dawson and his wife as well as Colby. Anything you want to say?"

Holloway looked at the floor and then with a smirk and venom in his voice said, "I got nothin' to say. But you can't pin that murder on me. That one in Laredo. Yeah, I did it but there is more to it."

"There's nothing more to it," said John. "You killed her and left a boy without his mother. I'm gonna see you pay for what you've done. But I'm not gonna put up with much from you. If you don't want to go to Laredo, you can join your friends in the cemetery."

John tied Holloway to the hitching rail in front of the store. "Nicks, you reckon we could camp on your porch for this evening? I'll be heading out at first light for Laredo."

"Of course you can, John. Make sure he's tied up and I'll get you some canned beans and peaches. Seems to me I remember you bein' partial to 'em."

"Good memory. I do like 'em. Nicks, I'll need some more groceries for my trip. If you will gather us enough food for both of us to last four days. That should be enough to get us to Laredo. Fortunately, Holloway has plenty of money to pay for it. Also, go through the saddle bags on all three of their horses. Gather any money you find and I'll take that in. Then for Gomez and Atkins' horses, they won't be needing them anymore. As far as I'm concerned, you can have them and their saddles.

"Thanks, John. I'll take good care of them. I've got one other thing I think you could use for your trip." Nicks went to the back of his store and came back with a set of leg irons. "Do you think you could use these?"

"Well, Nicks. You told me last time I was here that had just about everything in your store. You have proved that to be true."

"This pair has an extra-long chain that comes apart in the

middle. That's so you can use them while he's riding his horse. Once he is in the saddle, you just connect the two chains under the horse's belly."

"You're not gonna keep me trussed up all the way to Laredo are you?" asked Holloway.

"I will unless you cause trouble. Then you'll get thrown across your saddle and I'll chain your hands and feet together."

"That just ain't human," said Holloway.

"You mean, 'humane,'" John replied. "You're right. That's the way to take care of wild animals. Only a wild animal would murder people. You are nothin' more than an animal. Don't give me cause to use other measures on you. But if you do, you can know I'll be ready to accommodate you."

Holloway actually shuddered at John's cold words. He could tell the diminutive cowboy meant everything he said.

* * *

When morning came, John opened another can of beans and fed some to Holloway.

"Nicks, if you'll help me, I want to get him in the saddle and get started."

Nicks helped Holloway into the saddle as John connected the leg irons under his horse.

"At least cuff my hands in the front. I can't ride with them in the back."

"They're stayin' right the way they are. Nicks, thanks for takin' care of the buryin' of Holloway's friends. As far as I'm concerned, you can just roll 'em in a hole and put dirt on 'em. They don't deserve anything more."

John took the reins of Holloway's horse and swung up onto Midnight.

Roy Clinton

CHAPTER 21

Holloway's horse followed closely behind Midnight. They made it to Moore by dusk. At the saloon, John swung down and tied both horses securely.

"Ain't you gonna get me down," yelled Holloway as John went inside.

John ordered a beer and told the bartender he had captured Holloway. The bartender told others that were in the bar. Soon they were all outside gawking and the man who had caused trouble there just a few days before.

"You want us to take care of him for you?" asked the bartender.

"Depends on what you mean by takin' are of him. If you mean gettin' him off his horse, I'd 'preciate the help. But if you mean something more...."

The bartender laughed. "Come on men. Get this lowlife off his horse. Chain him up on the porch. I guess I need to get him somethin' to eat."

"That would be fine. Just tell me how much it costs and I'll take care of it."

"And I want a drink, too," yelled Holloway. The bartender

turned around and laughed.

"Is there a place where I can bed down for the night?" asked John.

"I've got a room upstairs you can use. What do you want me to do with Holloway?"

"Tell you the truth, I'm more concerned with him escapin' than anything else. I think he will be better chained outside where he can be seen."

"That sounds fine with me," said the bartender. "I'll have your horses taken care of for the evenin'. Just leave it all to me."

The bartender passed on orders to a couple of the men who were drinking. They got up and went out to take care of the horses. John ate dinner and went upstairs, glad to be out of the saddle. He knew all the time on horseback was taking a toll on him. But he knew he would be in Laredo soon.

When morning came, the bartender served breakfast to John and Holloway. The bartender helped John get Holloway back on his horse and the leg irons secured.

"You can't make me spend another day chained up like an animal." Holloway bellowed and cursed as he was put on his horse. John paid the bartender for the food and the room and left him an extra five dollars for his help in taking care of Holloway.

All the way to Frio City, Holloway complained. He said he was tired of being in the saddle and he took exception to being chained the whole trip. John just smiled each time he complained and ignored him.

Once in Frio City, John went to the sheriff's office, and had

Holloway locked up and made arrangements for him to have a meal. He then went to the telegraph office and sent a message to Slim.

Richard Hanson

Bandera, Texas

Captured Holloway. Bring Richie and meet me in Laredo for trial.

John Crudder

Frio City, Texas

John went to the café, had a meal and contemplated the rest of his journey. He wanted to make it to Darlington by dusk so he decided to cut lunch short and get started. When he got to the jail to collect Holloway, he was met with complaints and profanity from his prisoner.

"I haven't even finished eating. And this is the first time I'm been out of handcuffs since we started. The deputy wouldn't even take off my leg irons. You don't have to treat me like this."

John continued ignoring Holloway and accepted the help of the sheriff and deputy to put Holloway on his horse. Once they got him in the saddle, they connected the chains of his leg irons and John headed for Darlington.

✻ ✻ ✻

Just before dark, John pulled into Darlington and swung down in front of the store.

"John!" shouted Etta Mae. "I'm so glad to see you again! Thank you so much for the sideboard. It's—what's he doing here?"

"Hello, Etta Mae," said Holloway. "Don't you have any kind words for your brother-in-law? I hope you have something good for supper. I recall you are a wonderful cook."

"Don't speak to me, you animal. Did you forget you stole from us when you were here?"

"Easy, Etta Mae," said Holloway. "Why does everyone call me an animal? I'm just a poor misunderstood cowboy who is tryin' to make a go of it in the world."

"Hello, John," shouted Hubert from the barn. Then he lowered his voice. "I had hoped I wouldn't see you ever again, Percy."

"Is that any way to talk to your own brother?"

"You're not my brother. I don't claim any kin to you," said Hubert. "But you owe me fifty bucks for all you stole when you were here last."

"I don't owe you nothin'," shouted Holloway with anger in his voice.

John swung down and went to his saddlebag to remove some money. "Hubert, the good news is Percy had plenty of money on him when I captured him. Here is the fifty dollars he owes you."

"Thanks, John. What happened to Gomez and Atkins?" asked Etta Mae.

"They are buried back in Nicksville."

"I wish Percy had been buried with them," said Hubert.

"Now brother. You need to have more respect for me."

"I have no respect for you," said Hubert. "It won't be long 'til you are hanged in Laredo and buried there."

Holloway kept silent as he contemplated the truth of his brother's statement.

"Hubert, can you help me get your brother out of the saddle? I'm still finding my arm a bit stiff and sore."

"Sure thing, John."

"Come on in, John," said Etta Mae. "I've got supper ready. But I don't want that man in my house."

"He can eat on the porch," said Hubert. "John help me get him chained to the corner post."

"You can't treat me like that," yelled Holloway. "I'm a man! You need to treat me like one."

"You're wastin' your breath," said John. "You haven't cared about anyone but yourself. Now, I'm gonna make sure you're always kept out in the open where I can see you."

Holloway grumbled and cursed. As John and Hubert went in for supper, Percy started beating his chains against the window and yelling that they needed to let him come inside. Etta Mae picked up a frying pan and went out to the porch.

"If you break my window, I'm going to crown you with this frying pan. And if you keep yelling, I'll use this to quiet you down. Got it?"

Holloway stopped the noise and sat quietly on the porch. Subconsciously, he rubbed his head where Nicks had hit him with his frying pan. He never made another noise during the evening. When their meal was over, Etta Mae took a plate of food out to

Holloway and fed him since his hands were cuffed behind his back.

"Thank you, Etta Mae. I knew you were a good Christian woman."

"Don't you say another word to me, Percy. If you do, I'll take the rest of your supper inside." Holloway immediately stopped his talking. He was sure his sister-in-law was not making an idle threat.

After supper, Etta Mae cleared the dirty dishes and brought bandage materials, whisky, and ointment. John knew what was coming. He pushed his chair back from the table as Etta Mae unwrapped the bandage from his head. She shook her head and repeated grunts that showed her displeasure in how the wound was healing.

Without any protest John removed his shirt so she could get to the wound in his arm. As she was finishing with that wound, Hubert pulled his chair up to John's and reached down for John's boots. Without any conversation, John raised his foot and Hubert removed his boot. Then John raised his other foot and Hubert removed it as well. On cue, Etta Mae turned her back and John slipped off his pants but held them close to cover himself as best he could. In a few minutes Etta Mae had changed the dressings and applied ointment.

"John, you're not going to like this but you are not healing up like you should. And as long as you keep riding as hard as you have, you're not going to heal. You have to take it easy or you run the risk of having more problems than just some extra holes in your body."

*　*　*

As the sun began to come over the horizon, John had the horses saddled. Hubert wanted to help but John stubbornly went ahead and saddled both horses saying he would accept only help getting Holloway into the saddle.

He didn't want to admit it to himself but John's wounds were causing him a great deal of pain. Etta Mae was right about him needing to take it easy. He decided he would go no further than Cotulla that day.

John had Midnight walk throughout the day. The amazing stallion didn't try to move faster. It was as if Midnight could sense John's discomfort. Unfortunately, Holloway could also see that John was struggling. Just before noon, Holloway made his move.

Holloway spurred his horse beside Crudder and used his forehead to butt John on his scalp wound. He used his head as a hammer and pounded John twice before John knew what had happened. John fell from the saddle unconscious. Holloway tried to urge his horse forward so he could reach the reins John had tied to his saddle.

Midnight immediately sensed what had happened and moved forward, pulling Holloway's horse with him.

"Come back here you blame horse," yelled Holloway. Midnight stopped, turned back and bit Holloway on his leg. Holloway let out a wail. Midnight bit him again and Holloway started crying.

"Get away from me, horse. Please don't bite me again."

Midnight relented and went back to where his owner had fallen. The horse nuzzled John and gently massaged his face. In a few minutes, John regained consciousness. As he sat up, he realized his head wound had ripped open. Blood had pooled on the ground. He pulled off his neckerchief and tied it tightly around his head. The pain was much greater as he did so, but he knew if he continued to lose blood, he would not survive.

"Look what your horse did to me!" cried Holloway. "I think he's ruined my leg. I didn't know horses could bite that hard. I'm bleedin'. Do something."

John pulled himself onto his horse and decided he would respond to Holloway's request and 'do something.' He pulled his gun and brought the barrel down on Holloway's nose. Blood gushed from the wound.

"What are you doin'? You can't do that to me." John turned back to Holloway and held up his gun again. "Please don't hurt me again. I'll be good."

John moved ahead with Holloway's horse following close behind. They made it to Cotulla by nightfall.

CHAPTER 22

As he rode up to the hitching rail in front of the dining hall, several hands came out and hurled insults at Holloway. It was clear they had reason to hate him. John recalled how Joe talked about Holloway and his friends being lazy and getting into fights. No doubt, many of the hands had to pick up the slack from Holloway's laziness.

Before John could get off his horse, word had gotten to Joe that they had company. "Hello, John. I see you've got that no-account sidewinder with you. Where are his friends? John, what happened to you? You have blood all down your shirt."

As John started to move from the saddle, several cowboys stepped forward to help him down and ease him into the dining hall.

"Hello, Joe. Holloway got the drop on me back on the trail. Used his head like a batterin' ram and busted my head open. I just need to get this cleaned up a bit and get somethin' to eat."

"We better get your head looked at first. Somebody go get Mo and tell him to bring his doctorin' kit." The hands half carried John to the back of the dining hall and laid him on a cot that was set up against the wall. Mo came over with a bucket of medical supplies.

"John, you shor messed up your head," said Mo.

"Actually, Holloway did that. He's the one who shot me to begin with. Then he busted my head open again usin' his own hard head."

"He did a good job. I'm gonna have to stitch that up again. All of the stitches have torn out."

"When you finish with me, I think Holloway's nose will need some attention. He got in the way of my gun barrel after he busted my head."

Mo laughed. "Yup, it looks like he got taught a bit of a lesson."

"Also, you need to look at his leg. I think Midnight took exception when he knocked me out of the saddle. It looks like Midnight got in a few good bites on his leg."

Mo laughed again. "Sounds like a good horse. I'll check on Holloway after I get you stitched up."

Joe was watching Mo work and spoke to John. "So what happened to Gomez and Atkins?"

"They're bein' buried in Nicksville. And if ole man Nicks hadn't hit Holloway with a fryin' pan, they'd be burin' him too."

Joe doubled over with laughter. "I shor would have liked to have seen that. Come on boys. Go out and get Holloway down and chain him up in the yard. I don't want to waste any good groceries on him. See if Mo has any scraps he can feed him."

"I'm not eatin' any scraps. I'm not a dog," said Holloway.

"That's where you're wrong," said Cotulla. "You are a dog. And it don't make me no matter whether you eat or not. Boys, make sure you get his chains good and tight."

Mo finished up with John and went out to tend to Holloway's wounds. Joe helped John off the cot and walked him to a table. "We were just finishin' up supper. Mo's made chicken and dumplings. I think you'll like 'em."

"I'm sure I will. So far, I've liked everything Mo's made."

"John, I've made a decision. I'm ridin' with you to Laredo. And I'm bringin' a couple of hands with me. I don't want to take a chance on Holloway gettin' the drop on you again. You really ought to stay here on the ranch but I know you won't do it."

"No, I won't stay behind but I'll sure take you up on your offer to ride with me. I think I can make it fine but I don't have a lot of energy left-over to deal with Holloway."

"My suggestion is that we wait around here tomorrow and let you get your strength back," said Joseph. "We can leave the next day and make it down to Laredo in two days."

"Actually, that sounds good to me. I can use the rest," said John. And when we head out, we need to stay away from Encinal. Holloway murdered three people there. If I bring him through that city, they'll not let me take him on further. I need to get him to Laredo. Slim's bringin' his son Richie down there to see the murder trial."

"I'll be glad to see Slim again," said Joe. "We have a lot of catchin' up to do."

"I'm sure he'll be glad to see you as well. Joe, if you don't mind, I think I'll skip supper. I think I'd like to lie down. At this point, I think sleep will do me more good than food."

"Sure, John. Let me help you over to be bunkhouse. And tomorrow, you stay in when the hands get up. Sleep as long as you can and then Mo will get you something to eat."

"Thanks, Joe. I'll do that."

That night, John slept soundly and didn't even stir when the hands got up for breakfast. Somewhere around midmorning, John woke up, dressed and walked over to the dining hall. Mo was there as always.

"What would you like for breakfast? I can get you some bacon and eggs. Or I can make you some pancakes and sausage."

"Mo that all sounds good. But I don't reckon you have any of those chicken and dumplings left-over, do ya'?"

Mo smiled and said, "Just give me a few minutes to heat it up. And I've got some biscuits left from breakfast that will go well with it."

John took a seat and Mo filled a bowl with the delectable treat. As far as he knew, he had never had chicken and dumplings before but he was sure it would not be the last time. He expressed to Mo how much he liked them and that it was something new for him.

"I'll write down the recipe if you like. I'm sure that wife of yours will be able to make it for you any time you like." Mo disappeared into the kitchen and in a few minutes emerged with the recipe carefully notated. "I also wrote out my 'nana puddin' recipe, just in case you get a hankerin' for that and you can't get back to Cotulla." Mo laughed at his own joke and John smiled in response.

John ate what he could and excused himself to go back to the bunkhouse. He slept right on through until supper. His body was taking advantage of the opportunity to heal from the trauma of travel.

✳ ✳ ✳

Joe picked out two of his top hands to be in charge of seeing to Holloway. They got him breakfast, took him to the outhouse and then put him on his horse and connected the leg irons beneath his horse.

"There's plenty of you here so you don't have to worry about me escaping. Please take off these leg irons. And the hand cuffs are pulling my shoulders out of joint."

Joe and the other men just ignored Holloway. With great pain, John pulled himself into his saddle. Midnight moved ever so gently as if he understood he needed to be careful with John.

At the end of their first day out of the Cotulla Ranch, they had were about ten miles south of Encinal. John was glad they hadn't met up with anyone there. He would not have been willing to give up his prisoner and would have done whatever was necessary to keep him.

Toward evening on the second day, the group made their way to Laredo. John led the way to the sheriff's office, swung down, and went inside.

"Sheriff Lasiter," said John. "I've got a prisoner for you."

"Howdy, John. It's good to see you," said the sheriff as he got up and went out to the hitching rail. "Where's Gomez and Atkins?"

"They're back at Nicksville pushin' up daises."

"That'll just save us the trouble of two more trials."

"Just so you know. Holloway and his partners murdered three people in Encinal a few days ago. They wanted me to bring them back there when I found 'em but I told them Laredo had a prior claim."

"Don't worry about them," said Sheriff JD. "I'll handle things with their sheriff. They can have Holloway's body after he's tried and hung. They can do what they want with him."

John introduced Joseph Cotulla and the other men. After handshakes all around, Lasiter took charge of the prisoner and prepared to lock him in a cell.

"I'm gonna go find the judge. I told him you were gonna bring Holloway in. He said he wanted to put him on trial just as soon as possible. If you'll look around the side, you'll see the hangin' scaffold is almost finished. The judge got it started soon after you went after Holloway.

"Don't sound none like I'm gonna get a fair trial here," said Holloway. "That ain't right."

"Holloway, don't you worry about it," said JD. "We're gonna treat you a lot better than you did Marie Hanson. We're gonna give you a fair trial, give you a last meal, and then we will hang you by the neck 'til you are dead."

Lasiter's deputy led Holloway to his cell as Holloway loudly protested the way he was being treated.

"Sheriff Lasiter, there's one more matter. There's over a thousand dollars in my saddlebags that we took off Holloway and his gang. I've got a feelin' he has more loot from his bank jobs stashed. I don't know if it will ever be found."

"Let's get inside and get the money counted," said the sheriff. "I'll give you a receipt and then take it to the bank in the morning. Meanwhile, you all might as well get rooms at the hotel and have somethin' to eat. Usually the judge starts trials two days after we get a prisoner."

"That sounds good to me, sheriff," said John. "I could sure use the rest." John turned to Cotulla and said, "I think Slim should be here by tomorrow or the next day at the latest. I'll see you men in the morning. I'm going to bed."

John turned and mounted Midnight and headed to the livery stable. After giving him a good brushing and paying for his feed and board, John went to the hotel and paid for a room and a bath. When he made arrangements for the bath, the proprietor asked if he wanted to purchase a cigar to enjoy with his bath. John's stomach flipped with the mere mention of a cigar. He remembered how sick he got in San Antonio when he had a bath at the Menger Hotel and tried his first cigar. So far as he was concerned, that was his first and last.

Roy Clinton

CHAPTER 23

LAREDO, TEXAS

M onday morning, Judge William Moore had Sheriff JD Lasiter post a notice that the trial would take place the next morning. The poster said:

Here Ye, Hear Ye, Hear Ye
Judge William Moore has decreed that
Jasper "Percy" Holloway
will stand trial for the murder of
Consuelo Marie De Zavala Morales Hanson
on Tuesday, February 17, 1874 at 9 o'clock a.m.
All interested parties are instructed to be in court at that time.

John was concerned for he had not heard from Slim and Richie. He went to see Judge Moore to voice his concerns. Inside his office, John saw the judge was a tall, mature man with wavy, flowing gray hair. He had a distinguished face that spoke of many years working in the sun. John was impressed that the judge appeared to be someone who had not spent all of his time in court.

"Howdy, young man. What happened to your head?" asked Judge Moore. "Well Judge, I've got a problem."

"Now hold it right there, son. I don't even know your name."

"I apologize, Judge. My name is John Crudder and I'm…."

"Well John, it's nice to meet you. Now in court, people always address me as Judge Moore or just Judge. But in my office, I like to be on a first name basis. You may call me Snookey."

"I'm sorry, but I thought your name was William."

"Indeed it is. My momma used to call my brother Sonny so when I came along, she started callin' me Snookey. Don't know why she did it but the name stuck. I've been called Snookey ever since. Now I asked you what happened to your head? You got it all bandaged up."

"Judge—I mean, Snookey. I got shot by Holloway. He also shot me in my arm and my leg and left me for dead."

"That wasn't very neighborly of him now, was it?"

John scratched his head as he considered what the judge had said. "No, Snookey, it was not very neighborly. But I came here with another concern. I saw you're callin' for the trial of Holloway to begin in the morning. Sir, the problem is the key witness, Mrs. Hanson's son Richie, is not yet in town. I'm sure he's comin'. I sent word for him soon after I captured Holloway, but I don't see how the trial can proceed without a witness. At the very least, you will have to declare a mistrial. At worst, Holloway will be found not guilty due to an absence of evidence."

"John, you seem like you know a lot about the law. Are you a lawman?"

"No, sir. I was once the marshal of Bandera but by training, I'm an attorney."

"Well, John. That's really good news. I'm so glad you came in here today. Hold up your hand."

"What?"

"John this is an easy thing to do. Just hold up your hand." John lifted his left hand. "Not that one. I need your other hand."

John painfully lifted his wounded arm and had a feeling he was going to regret his visit to the judge.

"Do you solemnly swear you will faithfully execute all the duties of district attorney of Laredo, Texas, to the best of your ability, so help you God? Now say, 'I do.'"

"But Judge, I can't prosecute Holloway. I'm the one who brought him in. And I don't even live in Laredo."

"That don't matter. You don't have to reside in our fair city."

"But Judge—I mean Snookey. I protest. This simply is not right."

"Well, our district attorney is down in Mexico for the next two weeks so we need a stand in. You're it. Now I need to hear you say 'I do,' or I might need to find you in contempt of court.'"

John sighed deeply and shook his head. Knowing he didn't have any other choice, he said, "I do. But judge, I want to go on record as saying I protest this appointment."

Snookey smiled broadly. "I'm glad to have you as a member of the bar in Laredo, John. I forgot the best part. You get a salary of one dollar a day."

"Thank you, Snookey. If it's all the same to you, I would like to donate my salary to the city of Laredo. But, your honor, if Richie is not in town for the trial, I'm going to move for a postponement."

"You can make the motion if you want to. But we are goin' on with the trial in the mornin'. Sheriff Lasiter can testify. And the schoolmarm saw Holloway runnin' away. You have enough evidence to get a conviction. My own sainted mother could get a conviction with that evidence."

John turned and walked out of the office. He stood on the boardwalk, out front, wondering how he had gotten himself into such a mess. As he moved toward the hotel, he saw Slim and Richie walking toward the sheriff's office.

"Slim! Richie!" shouted John as he hobbled toward his family. "When did you get to town?"

"We got in late last night," said Slim. "We got a room hopin' we'd see you this mornin'. What happened to you?"

"Holloway and his gang shot me up and left me for dead. I've got Holloway in jail. I'm so glad to see both of you. The trial starts in the morning. I just came from the judge's office. He has ordered me to be the prosecutor."

"What!" exclaimed Slim. "How can he do that? Especially since you got bushwhacked by Holloway."

"I've just gone round and round with the judge. His head is set. I don't see as I have any choice."

"What happened to the rest of Holloway's men?" asked Slim.

"They didn't take kindly to me tryin' to serve a citizen's arrest.

They're buried in Nicksville." John turned from Slim to the young man with him. "Richie, I'm glad to see you. How are you doin'?"

"I'm fine, John. But I've got kind of a queasy feeling in my stomach. Just being back in Laredo brought back a lot of memories. Not all of them bad. But it reminds me of how lost I felt after I buried Ma."

Slim slipped his arm around his son and pulled him close. "Richie, oh how I wish we could bring your mother back. But I want you to know, you have family now. I'm always here for you."

"I know, Pa. I'm just sad…." His voice trailed off as he thought about the great void in his heart.

"Slim, I think I'd like to have some breakfast. Have you eaten yet?"

"Not yet. How about it, Richie? You ready to eat?"

Richie's face brightened. "Yes, I'm ready. I'll be glad to eat something more than Pa's cooking."

Slim smiled at his son's gentle jab at him. Together the three of them walked into the hotel dining room and were greeted by Joseph Cotulla.

"Slim!" shouted Cotulla from across the room. "How are you doing, old friend?"

"Joseph! It's so good to see you. How long's it been? Nine years? You were just a young pup then."

"And I thought you were such an old man," laughed Joe. "I'm thirty now. And the older I get, the younger you look."

Slim laughed, "Funny how the passin' of a few years changes our perspectives. I want to introduce you to my family. This is my son-in-law, John Crudder."

"Joe and I are old friends now," said John. "He and his men took care of me after I was shot up by Holloway. And I've had many meals in his dining hall. Slim, it looks just like the one on the H&F."

"I told you I liked that building, Slim." Joe smiled as he told Slim about the construction and how he copied just as much of it as he could remember after seeing the H&F Ranch.

Slim put an arm on Richie's shoulder and spoke to Joe. "And this is Richie. His mother was Marie. Joseph Cotulla, I would like for you to meet my son, Richie Hanson."

"I'm pleased to meet you, Mr. Cotulla."

"What a polite young man," said Joe. "I am so glad to meet you, Richie. Your father loved your mother with all his heart. When we were on the cattle drive from down in Mexico to Kansas City, Slim talked about how much he missed your mother. It had been about seven years since she told Slim she couldn't marry him. And he didn't know anything about you. But every day he talked about his love for your mother. I have to tell you, I got plenty tired if it. When we got to Kansas City, I was a happy man. Not just because the cattle drive was over but because I didn't have to hear the same stories from love-sick Slim."

Slim smiled at the memory. "He's right, Richie. I didn't have but a few short months with your mother but I loved her with all of my heart."

A tear came to Richie's eye. "I'm glad. I never knew why my father was not around. Ma never talked about you. I thought you had abandoned us but she told me that was not true. When I asked her what happened, she said she would tell me when I was older. But she never got around to telling me about you. And she never talked about her family. I know she had a younger brother but I never met him. We went to see them once but her mother wouldn't even let us get out of the wagon. She said mean things. Ma was hurt but she taught me it was not right to hate."

"I'm glad she did," said Slim. "Hating others is not right. Your mother raised you to be a fine young man. I'm sure she was very proud of you."

Richie wiped his eyes and said, "I'm hungry. Are we going to eat or what?"

All of the men laughed, grateful Richie had given them a way to move on in their conversation. Each ordered steak and eggs, a hotel favorite. The meals were served with tortillas, refried beans, and salsa picante.

When their meal was finished, they continued talking and laughing. John excused himself saying he had to prepare for the trial and meet with potential witnesses. Slim and Joe stayed in the dining room and continued to visit. Richie said he wanted to walk around town and see some friends.

When he left the hotel, Richie mounted Laredo and rode him down to the house where he was raised. He was surprised to find the front door open and several people inside. There were two women who were cleaning and moving furniture to the porch.

Richie swung down and walked up the stairs onto the porch. A large man wearing a black frock coat with a white shirt came out to meet him. Richie immediately recognized his mother's landlord.

"Mr. Bradshaw. What's going on?"

"Hello Richie. I'm so sorry about the death of your mother. She was a fine woman. A very fine woman."

"Thank you, Mr. Bradshaw. But what are you doing with our furniture?"

"Well, Richie. I'm sorry to say that we are going to sell it to pay the debt your mother owed."

"What debt? I know she always paid the rent on time. I know because she always gave the money to me and I brought it to you in your office. Don't you remember?"

"Now, now, Richie. You don't have to get huffy with me, young man. I agree that your mother paid the rent on time. But there is the fact that the rent hasn't been paid in two months. I even came here to see if I could help. That's when I found out that your mother was—that she was—that she died."

"She was murdered, Mr. Bradshaw."

"Yes, yes. As I was saying, I came here and found out about your mother and you were nowhere around. I have waited all of this time and no one has come forward to pay the rent. I have no choice but to seize the furniture and prepare the house to be rented by someone else."

"You have no right!" shouted Richie. He watched as a lady was swooning over the sewing machine his mother had used. "That belongs to my mother! Leave it alone. It is nearly brand new. She just got it."

The lady was stunned and backed away from the machine.

"You just wait 'til my Pa gets here. You'll wish you hadn't messed with Ma's things."

"Your Pa?" Bradshaw backed up a couple of steps and considered what Richie had said. "I didn't know you had a pa—I mean I never met your father."

Richie swung up onto Laredo and rode hard back to the hotel. He ran inside the dining room and yelled. "Pa! Come quick. Someone's trying to steal Ma's things."

Slim and Joe came out of the hotel following Richie. "They are at my house just down the road. Please hurry before they steal everything."

Richie mounted Laredo and rode quickly back to his house. As he passed the sheriff's office, Sheriff Lasiter and Crudder came outside to see what the commotion was all about. They watched Slim and Joe running after Richie's horse. John joined in with the running men. They had yet to saddle their horses so they ran as fast as they could. Meanwhile, Sheriff JD swung up and quickly caught up with Richie.

When Richie and the sheriff arrived, the woman was once again back inspecting the sewing machine and Bradshaw was helping her move it to a waiting wagon.

"What's goin' on here?" demanded the sheriff.

"He's stealing Ma's sewing machine and all of her furniture. He said she owed him money. But that's a lie."

"Now, now, son, let's calm down now," said Bradshaw.

"I'm not your son. Here comes my Pa now. Pa, this man is

stealing all of Ma's stuff."

"Now mister, I don't want you gettin' riled like this boy here. But I've got every right to her things. She owes two months back rent."

"I order you to stop this immediately," said John. "There has been no due process. If you're owed money, we'll find out soon enough."

"My name is Bradshaw and I own this house. And who are you, sir? And what gives you the right to order me to do anything?"

"My name is John Crudder and I'm the district attorney. Are you going to stop this immediately or do I have to go get Judge Moore and bring him down here? Or better yet, would you like for me to order Sheriff Lasiter to put you in jail?"

"Well, I…I…uh…I…well. I'll stop. I just needed to have things explained to me." Bradshaw looked like he was on the verge of tears.

Crudder walked onto the porch so he could face Bradshaw. The overdressed man looked down on John. "Now Mr. Bradshaw, why do you say Marie Hanson owes you money?"

"Because I haven't been paid since she died. I've got a right to take the abandoned possessions and sell them to satisfy her debt."

"Mr. Bradshaw, you sound like a heartless, moneygrubbin' skinflint to me. How much are you owed?" asked John.

"Fifty dollars," said Bradshaw. "The rent is twenty-five dollars a month."

"Here's your fifty dollars," said Slim as he selected several bills from his pocket. "Now when is the rent due again?"

"It will be due next Wednesday," replied Bradshaw.

"Well if we need the house after next Wednesday, I'll be back to settle up with you. Meanwhile, you get off the property 'cause you're trespassin'. One more thing before you go. Have you taken anything out of the house?"

"Just some of the furniture. That's all."

"Well, you better go and round it up and get it back here now," said Crudder. "Otherwise I'll swear out a warrant against you and get the sheriff to arrest you."

"I'd be more than happy to arrest him," said Sheriff Lasiter.

"No please, sheriff. I'll get the furniture all back. I know right where it is. I had just sold it."

"Is that right?" asked the sheriff. "How much did you get for it?"

"Well, I got seventy-five dollars for it."

"So let me get this right. You already got more than was owed you and you were trying to get more. Is that right?" asked Crudder.

"Yes, but you understand I was just doing what I thought was the right thing to do."

"You have an interesting way of conducting business. I think the District Attorney's office will be looking further into your business practices." Crudder stepped closer to Bradshaw. "You have until next Tuesday at noon, to have all of your business records brought by the District Attorney's office."

"Bradshaw," said Sheriff Lasiter, "I've heard the order given to you by District Attorney Crudder. If you don't comply with this order, you'll be arrested."

With those words, John, Slim, and Joe, turned to go. Richie and JD took the reins of their horses and joined the group walking back to the hotel. They walked in silence for several minutes. Then Richie started to giggle. As they neared the hotel, his giggling became louder. Finally the group stopped and stared at Richie.

"Richie, what's so funny?" asked Slim.

"I was just thinking how great it is to have a family like you all. And I was thinking I'd bet Mr. Bradshaw wishes he had never even owned that house."

The rest of the group joined in the laughing and together they walked into the hotel. Joe said, "Richie, I wish I had a family like yours too!"

CHAPTER 24

T uesday morning, Richie came down from his room to find Abe, Slim, and John in the dining room. They were drinking coffee but had not yet eaten. Presently, Sheriff Lasiter joined them.

"Howdy, Richie. Men," said JD. "I could sure use some coffee."

"Me too," said Richie. "Sorry I slept so long. The ride must have taken more out of me than I realized."

"Sit down, son," Slim replied. "You didn't miss much. We're just getting' ready to start on our second cup."

"John," said the sheriff, "when will my testimony take place?"

"Right now. I think I'm gonna start with you after my opening statement."

"What about me?" asked Richie. "When will I testify?"

"I think you will be the last to testify. After JD gets off the stand, I'm gonna call the schoolteacher and then I'll call you."

✳ ✳ ✳

The trial began Tuesday morning promptly at nine o'clock.

Both attorneys gave their opening statements and then John moved on with the state's case against Holloway. Crudder called Sheriff JD Lasiter to the stand. His testimony was quick and precise. After he was cross examined, John called his next witness.

"Your honor, the state would like to call Miss Amelia Carpenter." The schoolmarm got up from her chair and made her way to the front of the courtroom. When she arrived at the witness chair, the bailiff approached her and held the Bible in front of her.

"Please place your hand on the Good Book and swear to tell the truth."

"Yes," said Miss Carpenter. "I'll tell the truth." She turned to the judge and said, "You're honor, I never swear. I don't think it is proper. Besides, many of my students and former students are here today. What would they think about their teacher swearing?" Then she looked at the sheriff. "And JD you know, I never swear but I always tell the truth." JD just nodded in agreement.

"Miss Carpenter, dag nab it. If you won't swear to tell the truth, how would you feel about promising to tell the truth? Would that be all right with you?"

"Yes, that would be fine your honor. I can do that." Then looking the bailiff in the eye, she straightened her back, lifted her right hand high and said, "I promise to tell the absolute truth here today." The bailiff began to turn away when she added, "And I promise to tell the absolute truth every day."

Judge Moore rolled his eyes and said, "That's fine Miss Carpenter. Please take the stand."

As she was getting situated, John stood and walked in front of the witness stand. "Miss Carpenter, what is your occupation?"

"I am the headmistress of the Laredo Public School. A position I have held for the last twenty-eight years."

"And Miss Carpenter, did you know Mrs. Marie Hanson?"

"Yes, I did. In fact, the school is right across the street from where Mrs. Hanson lived. She used to bring cookies to school regularly. And sometimes I would go over and have tea with her while the children were at recess."

"And do you recall seeing and hearing anything unusual on the morning of December twentieth of last year?"

"Yes, I do. It was a Saturday afternoon and I was at the school getting my classroom ready for the next term. We had already dismissed for Christmas break and I wanted to have the room prepared for when the students came back in the New Year."

John tried to move her along a bit. "And what did you see and hear, Miss Carpenter?"

"Well, I had the door open so it could air out some. That was because several of the boys had snuck in there the evening before to smoke their cigarettes. They knew I would be in on Saturday and they knew I forbid them from smoking."

"That's fine, Miss Carpenter. So the door was open, can you tell us what happened?"

"I heard a gunshot, that's what. I know it was a gunshot. It was so loud. I walked to the door and looked out. That's when I heard Richie, (she pointed) that's Marie's son, Richie Hanson scream. Then I saw a mean looking man run out of the house and get on a grey horse and ride away in a hurry."

"Do you see the man who ran from the house in the courtroom today?"

"Indeed I do, Mr. Crudder. It was that man." She pointed to Holloway. "It was the defendant Jasper Holloway. I'll never forget him. He had a big silver star on his holster like a sheriff's star but I don't think he was ever a sheriff."

John continued his questioning. "Is there anything else that stood out to you about the person you saw running from the house?"

"Why, yes there was. He had his gun out. I saw he was holding it in his left hand and he had a spider drawn on the back of his hand. I'm sure it was a tattoo. And I don't abide tattoos. Anyone who would mark their skin like that would…."

John hurriedly interrupted her. "Thank you Miss Carpenter. No further questions."

"Mr. Holcomb," said Judge Moore, "you may question the witness."

Holcomb stood and pranced to the witness stand. He stuck his thumbs in the pockets of his vest and gazed into the distance. "Thank you, your honor. Miss Carpenter, you said you are a teacher at the Laredo school. Is that correct?"

"No, Lennie. That is not correct. You were never that good at listening. I said I was the headmistress of the Laredo Public School. Do you remember now?"

"Yes ma'am. And in your role as headmistress of the Laredo Public School, did you often work at the school on Saturday?"

"Now Lennie, I did when I needed to. And since the term had

just ended, I always had the practice of coming in on the first Saturday after classes ended to prepare for the next term. And Lennie, you know that has always been my practice."

"I'm sorry, I don't know what you're talkin' about."

"Lennie, you remember when you were my student, you were the one who got the other boys to help you fill the schoolroom with toad frogs after school ended on that Friday before Christmas. You knew I would be there the next morning."

Holcomb's face blanched and his mouth opened but no sound came out. There were giggles throughout the courtroom.

"You didn't think I knew that was you, Lennie. But I knew very well who put those frogs in the classroom. You were always causing trouble and getting other boys in trouble with you. I'm surprised you ever made a lawyer, Lennie. You never were a good student."

The courtroom erupted into laugher. Even the judge was laughing.

"Your honor," Lennie sighed in exasperation. "Will you please instruct the witness to answer the questions without the additional commentary?"

"Very well," said Judge Moore. "Miss Carpenter. Please refrain from telling any more stories about Lennie and what a poor student he was. Just answer the questions."

"Yes, your honor."

Holcomb approached the witness stand again but this time without the pomposity he had a few minutes before.

"Miss Carpenter, are you sure you saw the defendant leaving

the Hanson house?"

"Of course, I'm sure Lennie. You know my eyesight is sharp. Lennie, straighten your back and don't slouch. You were standing so straight just a few minutes ago."

The rattled attorney trudged on. "But how could you have seen the tattoo on the defendant's hand from across the street. Isn't it true that you saw the tattoo in the courtroom and just thought you saw it on the man who was running from the house?"

"No, Lennie that is not true. I saw it plainly. Just like I can plainly see the gravy stain on your white shirt. You know you should always use a napkin to cover your shirt during breakfast. Especially if you're coming to court that day."

There was loud laughter throughout the courtroom. The judge half-heartedly banged his gavel but he was laughing as well.

"Your honor, can you please instruct the witness to answer my questions?"

"I think she answered your question, Mr. Holcomb. You questioned her eyesight and she was pretty convincing in her answer. Do you have any more questions?"

"No, your honor." Holcomb dropped his head and returned to his seat.

"You may step down, Miss Carpenter."

"Thank you, your honor."

"Call your next witness, Mr. Crudder."

"The state would like to call Richard Hanson, Junior."

Richie got up and walked to the witness stand. After taking his oath, he took a seat in the witness stand.

John walked up to Richie and said, "Do you mind if I call you Richie?"

"No sir, I don't mind."

"Richie," John began, "please tell the court exactly what you saw on the day in question."

"I had been at work at the dry goods store and had just gotten home. As I got to the porch, I heard Ma. It was like she was screaming but it wasn't loud. I went inside and I saw that man with his hand across mom's mouth."

Richie pointed to the defendant.

"You're doin' fine, Richie." John walked closer to Richie for a moment and nodded at him to affirm him. "What happened next?"

"He shouted at Ma that he wanted to know where she kept her money."

"Did your mother keep a lot of money in the house?"

"No, sir. We didn't have a lot of money. She made just enough to pay the rent and buy groceries. That's why I was working at the dry goods store. I wanted to help her get ahead a bit before I went to college."

John pressed on. He knew the next part of his testimony would be the hardest but he needed to guide Richie through it. "So Richie, you testified you heard the defendant ask where your mother kept her money. What happened next?"

Tears began to flow from Richie's eyes as he shouted, "He shot her! That man shot her!

Richie pointed at the defendant, holding his position for several seconds.

Roy Clinton

"Now, Richie, is there any chance the man you shot your mother was someone other than the defendant?"

"No, sir. That's him. I saw his hat with the notches all on one side. He had on his holster with the silver star and he was holding his gun with his left hand. And I saw that spider on his hand. That tattoo."

"No more questions, your Honor."

Immediately Holcomb approached Richie and went on the attack. "Now, Richard, isn't it true that in the confusion you didn't get a good look at the man that shot your mother?"

"No, sir. I saw him clearly. It was that man."

"Now don't be hasty, son. Couldn't you be confused at what you saw? Isn't it possible you didn't see the face of the man who shot your mother? You just thought you saw the defendant?"

"No sir. That's not true. My eyesight is good. I know what I saw. It was Mr. Holloway who shot my Ma. I saw it and you'll not be able to make me say anything else."

Holcomb turned and walked back to his seat. "I have no more questions for the witness."

Judge Moore said, "You may step down, young man."

Crudder stood and said, "The state rests, your Honor."

"Mr. Holcomb," said the judge, "you may call your first witness."

Holcomb stood and faced the jury. "Your honor, I would like to call Mr. Jasper Holloway."

Holloway got up and walked to the witness stand. The bailiff approached and asked him to raise his hand and if he would swear to tell the truth.

"Yeah, I'll tell the truth," Holloway replied.

"Now, Mr. Holloway, you have been reported to have been in the home of Marie Hanson on December the twentieth. Isn't it true you were no where near Laredo on that date?"

"No, I was in Laredo and I was in her house."

Holcomb's mouth dropped open. He turned from the jury to face the defendant. "I don't think you understood what I was asking. Isn't it true…."

"Oh, I knew what you was askin'. I was there. I was in her house but it wasn't like anyone said it was. I tried to tell Crudder there was someone else who was responsible but he wouldn't listen to me. He just put hand cuffs and leg irons on me and hauled me in."

"Your honor." Holcomb turned to appeal to the judge. "May I have a moment to confer with my client to clear up the confusion?"

"Your client doesn't appear to be confused," said Judge Moore. "In fact I think the only one who's confused is you."

Holloway spoke up and addressed the judge. "I'm not confused, judge. And I've got somethin' that needs to be said. There was someone else involved who is responsible."

"Go ahead Mr. Holloway," said the Judge. "Tell the court what you need to say."

"It's true I was in Hanson's house. But it was her brother who told me to do it. He gave me twenty bucks to go rough her up some."

There was a loud murmur in the courtroom as several people whispered at once. The judge rapped his gavel several times and

Roy Clinton

called for order in the court.

"Please proceed Mr. Holloway. Tell us exactly what happened."

"Alejandro," said Holloway, "that's her brother, told me his parents were old and he wanted to inherit everything but he needed to get his sister out of the way first. He said she kept a lot of money in the house and if I could get it, he would split it with me. But I realized all he wanted was for me to kill her for him."

The courtroom exploded with noise as people talked loudly to each other about what they had just heard. As the judge rapped his gavel, a man stood up and walked slowly to the front of the courtroom. He pulled a gun and said, "I'm not going to let you smear my name." He raised his gun toward the defendant.

Judge Moore pulled a six-gun from beneath his robe and shot the disrupter in the middle of his chest. With his other hand, Judge Moore rapped his gavel on the bench. "Order, order I say. Bailiff, I charge this man with contempt of court and fine him ten dollars. Go over to his body and collect the money. And if he lives, I sentence him to three days in jail."

"He's dead, Judge," said the perplexed bailiff as he went through the dead man's pockets.

"In that case, the jail sentence is suspended." The judge rapped his gavel again. "Some of you men, drag his body out of here and go get the undertaker."

The courtroom was silent. The only sound was from the rowels of the spurs of the men dragging the body from the room. Many of the spectators had a look of surprise or shock. But several, including the prosecutor, looked solemn, almost indifferent. John got the feeling it was not the first time Judge Snookey Moore had pulled his pistol to administer justice in his courtroom.

Soon after the shooting, the judge dismissed the jury so they could deliberate. Less than fifteen minutes later they came back with a verdict of guilty. The judge decreed that Holloway would hang on Saturday morning at noon, providing he could get a hangman by then.

✳ ✳ ✳

Wednesday morning, Richie was waiting in the dining room when Slim and John came down for breakfast. Slim sat beside him and put his hand on his shoulder.

"How are you feelin', son?"

"I'm doing all right. I'm just glad the trial is over. I still can't believe Ma's brother is the one who wanted her to be killed."

"It is sad what people will do for money," said Slim. "That probably will not be the last time in your life you will see something evil done out of greed."

"Pa, I know we had planned on staying until after the hanging on Saturday, but I don't think I want to see it. I've seen enough killing. Would it be all right with you if we went home?"

"That would be fine with me," said Slim.

"Me too," said John. "We can get started as soon as we get a wagon for your furniture. Slim, I'll go buy a wagon and a team and then we can get the furniture loaded."

"That's fine, John." Slim turned to Richie. "I'm glad you don't want to stay for the hangin'. It is enough for you to know that the killer will pay for his crimes."

A couple of hours later, they had a wagon loaded with Richie's furniture and his mother's sewing machine. They tarped everything down just in case it rained before they got back to Bandera. John volunteered to drive the wagon since he wasn't looking forward to putting his healing body back in the saddle. He put Midnight's saddle and gear in the wagon and allowed his horse to follow the wagon without being tied.

"Pa, would it be all right if I lead us home? I've already been thinking about places for us to camp."

"That'll be fine, son. That will be just fine.

EPILOGUE

BANDERA, TEXAS

B ack on the H&F, Richie took delight in adding his mother's furniture to the big house where he and Slim lived.

"Richie," Slim said, "It gives me great pleasure to have you and your mother's furniture here. I loved your mom so much. Now when I look at the various pieces that she picked out, it is almost like a bit of her is here with us."

"I feel the same way, Pa. Would you mind if I gave Charlotte Ma's sewing machine? I know I'll never use it."

"I think that's a fine idea. It will not get any use here. Charlotte will be able to put it to good use."

While they were talking, John walked in.

"Good afternoon," said John. "Y'all have any coffee on?"

"Help yourself," said Slim. "You know there's always a pot on over here. But I'll bet that's not why you're here. You knew I'd have a fresh pot going."

"You got me right, Slim. I knew you'd have coffee." John smiled as he enjoyed ribbing his father-in-law. "I need to ask you a favor. I want to use your kitchen. I told Charlotte I was cookin' supper. I want to do it over here so it will be a surprise for her. But I'm gonna need the help of both of you."

"I'll help," said Richie.

"Count me in," said Slim. "So what are we havin'?"

"When I was at Cotulla's ranch, his cook gave me his recipe for his banana puddin', 'cept it called it 'nana puddin'. It took me a while to figure out what he was talkin' about. Anyway, I just came from town and brought back some banana's and sugar wafers. He also taught me how me makes his fried chicken and his mashed potatoes and gravy."

"That sounds fine with me," said Slim. "And if you want, I think you've always liked my biscuits. I could make a pan of those."

"That sounds good to me," replied John. "Richie, you reckon you can get two chickens dressed?"

"I can do that!" Then Richie stopped and put on his best Texas drawl, and said, "Yup. I shor can. I'll get that done directly."

John and Slim laughed and Richie smiled his biggest smile.

For the next couple of hours the three men worked on their dinner preparations. Slim got his biscuits ready to go in the oven. Richie brought in the chicken and followed John's instructions and made a batter using buttermilk and flour. Slim pealed the potatoes and got them on to boil. John finished the pudding and got it ready to put in the oven and then started frying the chicken.

It took several batches to get all the chicken ready. John then

216

tackled the gravy as Slim put his biscuits in the oven while Richie went over to the house by the river to get Charlotte and the twins. When they arrived Charlotte said she could set the table if Claire and Cora would help her. They enthusiastically followed their mom around the table, putting forks and knives where they were told.

Finally, the meal was ready so Richie held a chair for Charlotte as she got seated. The twins sat on pots that were placed in their chairs so they could reach the table.

"There's something I want to say before we start," said Richie.

"Charlotte, I'd like for you to have my Ma's sewing machine. I think she would have liked for you to have it."

"Why Richie!" exclaimed Charlotte. "I am honored. Thank you for that wonderful gift. I will enjoy making dresses for me and for the girls. And you never know, gentlemen, I may be making you some shirts, too."

Slim and John exchanged looks. They had seen the homemade shirts some men wore. They all had a decidedly feminine look to them.

"Uh, honey," said John, "you don't need to worry about us. You spend all of your efforts making clothes for you and the girls."

"I agree, sweetheart," said Slim. "We'll do just fine. You make clothes for you and the twins."

Both men breathed a sigh of relief that they had narrowly dodged an uncomfortable conversation. With the food on the table, all took a seat and Slim looked out at his family.

"Before we eat, I think we ought to say grace."

Charlotte nodded in response and held out her hands and grabbed the hands of her daughters who were seated beside her. John and Slim reached out and took Richie's hands and then took the other hands of the twins. When their heads were bowed, Slim spoke.

"Lord, I just want to thank you for my family. You have blessed me with a fine daughter and two fine sons and two wonderful granddaughters. This is more than I ever deserved." Then he paused and tears dripped from his eyes. "And you have let me love two good women. I don't know why they had to be taken from me. But that's not for me to question. I just thank you for letting me love them." Charlotte, Richie, and John all teared up as they listened to Slim.

When Slim finished, Cora and Claire were both beginning to cry. "Why is everyone crying?" asked Cora.

"Is it because the chickens got dead?" asked Claire.

The adults couldn't help but laugh. Charlotte turned to her daughters and said, "It's all right girls. No, we're not sad about the chickens. We are just sad about Richie's mom and your grandmother dying. But we're not sad any more. We're happy because we have the two of you. Now who wants the first piece of chicken?"

"I do, I do," said the twins in unison.

The End

ACKNOWLEDGMENTS

First, I want to thank my wife Kathie who always has the first read of my books and makes so many helpful suggestions. Laredo as home of Richie and Marie was her idea. She lobbied hard for Marie not to die. (Most of her suggestions are gentle. And if I'm a bit slow on the uptake—as with the title for this book—she can make the suggestion a bit more forcefully so I finally get it. Thanks Kat!)

Then I want to thank my faithful beta readers. This group of incredible people read this book before others and make suggestions and corrections that make this a better book. This group includes: Teresa and Phil Lauer, Richard Barnes, Philip Placzek, Chris Bryan, and Michael Porter. Thanks so much for your helpful suggestions! (If you are interested in being a beta reader, please email me directly at Roy@TopWesterns.com.)

Once again, I have borrowed the names of friends and family members for this story. Snookey Moore has been a friend for more than twenty years. I had a good time envisioning him as the pistol-packing judge. The sheriff of Laredo has the name of my grandson JD Lasiter.

And Amelia Carpenter, a relatively new friend, has a classic name from the old west so I couldn't resist borrowing it for this book. I wrote much of one of the previous books on a tour bus as Amelia along with my wife and I enjoyed sightseeing on a trip to Spain and Portugal. Unlike the character in the book, she is happily married and is not a schoolmarm.

Joseph Cotulla was the founder of the city that bears his name. His character is portrayed as historically accurate. A favorite eating-place in Cotulla is Uncle Mo's Cafe. While I have not met Uncle Mo, my wife and I did enjoy a wonderful meal there with local residents. I borrowed his name for the cook on Cotulla's ranch, known as "the most popular man on the ranch" because of his great cooking.

While I never met Ruby, I did meet the inspiration for her character on a research trip to south Texas. She is portrayed exactly as she presented herself to us at a little hamburger stand in a small city (that will remain unnamed) in south Texas. My wife and I talked about what a wonderful and unique character she was for the next hundred miles.

Etta Mae is the name of my paternal grandmother who died before I was born.

For readers who are not fortunate enough to have been born in or now live in Texas, I would encourage you to get to Texas as soon as you can. Pick a city, rent a car, and drive out into the most beautiful country God has created. Stop in all of the small towns and enjoy the local color, along with the local eateries. Find out about the history of the town and get to know some of the residents. However, I must warn you; if you do this, you do so at your own peril. You may find yourself quitting your job and moving to Texas. Not that your move would be a bad thing. Just be aware, your trek to our great state comes with a wonderful unintended consequence.

I'm always glad to hear from readers. You may email me at Roy@TopWesterns.com. I make it a point to answer every letter. Please be patient if it takes me a few days to respond. I may be on a writing retreat or traveling but I will reply.

The next book in the *Midnight Marauder* series will be released soon. The title is *Bad to the Bone*. You may read a preview on the next few pages.

Roy Clinton

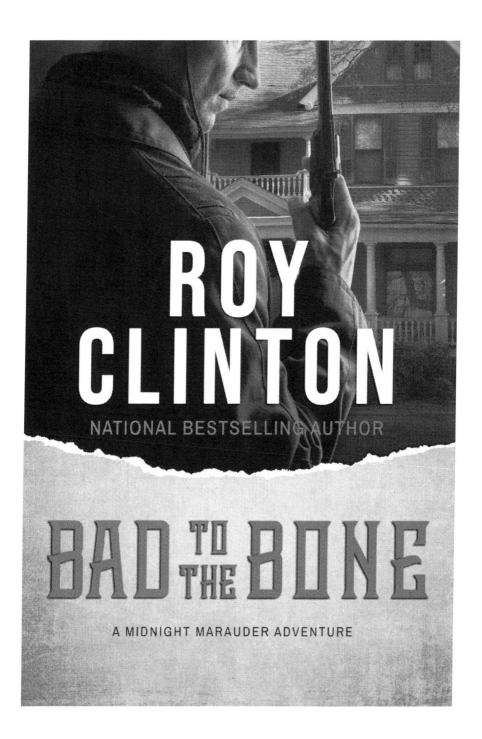

ROY CLINTON

NATIONAL BESTSELLING AUTHOR

BAD TO THE BONE

A MIDNIGHT MARAUDER ADVENTURE

BAD TO THE BONE

Roy Clinton

PREFACE

May 1874
Bandera, Texas

P lease don't hurt my husband anymore." Thelma Jamison watched in horror as Butch "the Butcher" Granger stomped on her husband's hand. Jack Jamison shrieked as he pulled back his mangled paw.

When Granger talked, his top lip was pulled back exposing his teeth. He appeared to have a permanent smile. His hair was gray and he wore long sideburns. While he didn't wear a beard, he did have a week's worth of whiskers that caused his face to appear dirty. Granger had big ears that stuck out from his head giving him an elf-like presence. His ample gut hung over his belt completely obscuring the buckle. Wide suspenders attached to his trousers accomplishing the herculean task of keeping his pants up.

"Where is it? I know you have gold hidden on your ranch. Everybody knows it. Old man you better tell me now. I'm runnin' out of patience."

"We don't have no gold mister. I'm just a worn-out old farmer.

I ain't never had more than fifty dollars to my name."

"Everyone in Bandera knows you're rich. You've been sittin' on a pile of gold all your life. Now where is it?" Granger took off Jamison's belt and looped it around Jack's other hand and dragged him roughly across the room. Thelma ran to her husband's aid and tried to pull the belt away from Granger. Butch pushed the elderly woman to the ground. As he stood over her, he took his six-gun from its holster, pulled back the hammer and shot Thelma in the middle of her forehead. Jack cried out and tried to crawl to his wife.

"Thelma! Thelma! What have you done mister? Why did you shoot Thelma?"

"You better tell me where your gold is or I'll kill you too."

Jamison let out loud wails as he looked at his dead wife. "All right. I'll tell you. There's a little strongbox buried in the barn. Please don't hurt me no more."

"Show me. Get up old man and show me where you have your gold."

Jack Jamison wiped his eyes as he stood. He walked over to the body of his wife and bent to kiss her. Granger savagely kicked the old man to the ground.

"I said show me where you buried the gold." Granger grabbed the belt and started dragging the old man out of the house.

"Please mister, let me walk. I'll show you where I it's buried."

Jamison got to his feet and staggered off of the porch and across the yard to the barn. He walked to the back of the barn and pointed to a barrel. "I buried it under this here barrel."

"So dig it up." Granger found a shovel and threw it at the feet of the old farmer.

Jamison used his uninjured hand to roll the barrel out of the way and began digging. After a few minutes, Granger lost patience with the slow progress, grabbed the shovel, and pushed Jamison to the ground. Granger dug down a little over two feet when the shovel struck the box containing the gold. After a few minutes later, Granger had freed the box from its hiding place. When he dragged it out of the hole, he opened it and found it filled with gold coins. On closer inspection, Granger realized the coins were all Double Eagles with dates from 1849 to 1866.

"How many you got?" asked Granger as he lifted out a handful of the Liberty Head coins.

"There are five hundred in that box and a few more in the cookie jar in the kitchen. That's over ten thousand dollars mister. You can have it if you will just ride away and leave me in peace."

"I can have it all right because it's mine now. And I'll be riding away just as soon as I put the gold in my saddlebags."

Granger pulled his gun from its holster and pulled back the hammer. With a sinister grin, he shot Jack Jamison twice in the chest. Granger retrieved his saddle bags, emptied them of the supplies he carried, and divided the gold coins between them. He guessed each bag weighed a little over fifteen pounds. Granger looked through the discarded supplies and retrieved the two sticks of dynamite he kept for what he called "special occasions." He walked to the house lit the fuse on both sticks, threw them inside and ran back to the barn.

The explosion was deafening but Granger was not worried about being caught. He knew the closest ranch house was a couple of miles away. Even if someone heard the blast he knew he would be long gone before anyone showed up at the ranch.

Butch Granger grew up in Bandera and was known for his cruelty. When he was only five years old, the marshal rode out to his parent's ranch and saw young Butch hacking up a dog with a long knife. The marshal swung down to scold the boy and discovered the remains of another dog. Granger's parents laughed it off when the marshal told them of their son's actions. "Boys will be boys" was all his father said.

No one recalls Butch's given name. When he started school, the other kids called him The Butcher because of his fondness for killing pets. They eventually shortened it to Butch. The moniker stuck. Butch liked the name and the reaction of people when they found out about his fondness for murdering small animals.

Granger left town when he was fifteen. His parents died in a fire that was of suspicious origin. It was assumed Butch started the fire but no one knew for certain. As far as anyone knew, Butch Granger never again came to Bandera until he killed the Jamison's, blew up their home, and rode away with their life savings.

END OF PREVIEW

I need your HELP!!

Willing to write a review on Amazon?

Here's how :
1) go to amazon.com
2) search for Roy Clinton
3) click on appropriate title
4) write a review

The review you write will help get the word out to others who may benefit.

— Thanks for your help,
Roy Clinton